ALICE, I THINK

SUSAN JUBY

Alice, I Think

Harper*Trophy* Canada
An imprint of HarperCollins*Publishers Ltd*

DISCLAIMER

This is a work of fiction. The characters are fictional, and any resemblance to anyone living or dead is a strange coincidence.

National Library of Canada Cataloguing in Publication

Juby, Susan, 1969-
Alice, I think / Susan Juby.

ISBN 0-00-639287-3

I. Title.

PS8569.U324A7 2003   jC813'.6
C2003-900496-1
PZ7.J858Al 2003

HC 9 8 7 6 5

Printed and bound in the United States
Typography by Alison Donalty
Set in Lynton

For my uncle and godfather,
Greg McDiarmid,
who always laughs in the right places and
who lived to see it

ACKNOWLEDGMENTS

In the beginning the goal was to make two funny people laugh: my uncle Greg and my friend Abbie Weinberg. They did, and I thank them.

Eternal gratitude also to:

Bill Juby for his patience, advice, and encouragement;

My mother, Wendy Banta, who survived my teen years and is now almost able to laugh about it;

James Waring, a solid-gold original;

Rod MacIntyre, Jesse Stothers, and the rest of the people at Thistledown for first taking a chance;

W. P. Kinsella for his vote of confidence;

Hilary McMahon for her belief;

My editor, Ruth Katcher, whose support, enthusiasm, and insightful questions have been invaluable;

Sandra Thomson; Elizabeth Murphy; Karl and Gail Hourigan; Aaron, Scott, and Carl Banta; Trevor Juby; Jessica McDiarmid; Terry, Ian, and Chris McDiarmid; Ian McDiarmid (the elder) and

Glenda (Eagle-Eye) Wilshire; Steve Vorbrodt; and
Robert Bringhurst for help of various kinds;

and a special nod to Frank for waiting
patiently in the car and under the desk.

ALICE, I THINK

WHEN I WAS SMALL AND ORDINARY,
BUT ALSO SPECIAL . . .

July 14

I blame it all on *The Hobbit.* That, and my supportive home life.

I grew up in one of those loving families that fail to prepare a person for real life. When I was little, my parents, especially my mother, encouraged me to be creative. She taught me to sing and dance, preferably on a table so everyone could get a good look. I could belt out show tunes and feminist anthems like "I Am Woman" by the time I was four. My parents would clap and cheer and make me feel like my talents and I were incredibly lovable.

"Come here," they'd say to their friends. "You've got to see Alice's new routine."

Then I'd get up on the table in one of my outfits and sing some totally inappropriate song at the top of my lungs.

I loved the attention. They loved the entertainment. I had no idea that it would spell my destruction.

They were practically sick with pride when I learned to read early, and they made sure I got a full set of all the classics. My favorite, although I didn't really understand it and my dad had to read most of it to me, was *The Hobbit.*

We talked a lot about the characters, and somewhere along the line I became convinced I was a hobbit. My parents loved this best of all. How incredibly creative and unusual this offspring of theirs was! Not only did they encourage me in thinking I was a hobbit, my mother actually made me a hobbit outfit. It included a burlap-sack tunic with twine fringe, brown felt slippers with bits of fake fur on the toes, and a pointy green hat. I wore it everywhere. I said hobbity things and practiced my deep, fruity laugh. I asked people to call me Took and carried an oversized pipe that my dad's friend picked up for me at something called a head shop. I liked to tell people that I was fond of flowers. And then my parents sent me off to school.

My parents didn't send me to kindergarten, because they said they didn't feel ready yet. But then my brother, MacGregor, was born, and they had to spread around their urge to overprotect. So off I went for the first day of first grade, where I quickly discovered that everyone else had bonded and figured out the rules the year before. My next discovery was that kids don't like other kids who think they are hobbits, especially kids who break into song and dance without any warning. In fact, as it turned out, there is probably no worse thing to be in first grade than a newcomer who thinks she's a hobbit.

Parenting Rule No. 1: Don't send your kids to school dressed like a character from a fantasy book unless that kid has a lot of friends who also dress like fantasy characters.

When the little blond girl came up to me and asked me

what I was supposed to be, I told her, even though some part of me dimly sensed it was a bad idea.

"I'm a hobbit," I announced proudly.

"What's that?" she asked, her little face intent. Maybe she was going to be my first friend at school. My mother told me school was where I was going to meet all kinds of kids who would be my friends and possibly also dancing partners.

"It's from this book called *The Hobbit*. It's really good."

"You read?" asked the girl.

I was breezy. "Oh yeah. Everyone our age does, practically."

Her face took on a look any less sheltered kid would have recognized as dangerous. But I didn't see it.

"So you're a what?" she asked.

"I'm a hobbit. We are small and ordinary but also special. We can be sort of invisible sometimes. And we laugh like this." I gave her my deepest and fruitiest laugh.

"You know what I think?" she asked.

I shook my head.

"I think you look like an ugly boy."

I took off my pointy hat and put my hand to my hair.

"And just so you know, ugly-boy girls like you can't have friends," continued the little blond girl.

Behind the girl stood six or seven other girls, all staring at me too. Accusing.

"I don't like you. No one likes you, even if you are a bobbit or whatever. And no one will ever like you."

And with that the little blond girl turned and left me

standing by myself on the playground, hobbit hat in hand, burlap sack filled with extra cakes for new friends over my shoulder.

Turned out that Linda, the little blond girl, was right. No one in my new classroom liked me. The other lonely kids were too scared by Linda and her gang to talk to me, even after I started wearing civilian clothes. By the end of the second week, picking on me had become the favorite activity. After the kids played dodgeball with me as the target, and bologna sandwiches as the ammo, I was afraid to go onto the playground. The playground monitors didn't seem to notice. Or maybe they didn't care. I overheard one refer to me as "that little delusional in the gunnysack." Good thing she was just in charge of the play yard and not the actual classroom.

My mom eventually had to come in to meet with the principal after I refused to leave the classroom at recess because Linda told me that she and her friends had "special plans" for me. Linda and I were sent to the office, and I had to sit there, two chairs away from my archnemesis, and listen to my mother yell at the principal.

"My God, don't you know what those kids are doing to my daughter? To her spirit? Don't you care?" my mother demanded.

The principal mumbled something.

"No. No!" My mother's voice rose. "She does not! She has come home crying every day since she started school. What's wrong with these kids? They act like animals! What's wrong with their families?"

I snuck a glance at Linda and saw that she was staring straight ahead.

Now I could hear the principal's voice too.

"Alice came to school dressed like an elf, Mrs. MacLeod. It wasn't Halloween. Children notice these things."

"A hobbit." I corrected him from my seat in the hall-way. Linda scowled at me.

"Can't she express herself?" screamed my mother. "She's just a little girl, for God's sakes!"

Linda's dad was called too. I can still remember the funny, sour smell he gave off when he brushed past me and, without saying a word, grabbed Linda by the arm and hauled her away. As he pulled her, I caught a glimpse of her face and saw for the first time that Linda didn't look so old after all. When her eyes met mine, she hardened her face and mouthed, "You're dead!" at me.

A week later Linda and her friends followed me home throwing rocks. One of the rocks hit me on the head and made me bleed. And that was the end of regular school for me. My mother and father have taught me at home ever since, which hasn't exactly set me on the road to being voted most popular but may have saved my life. And it also seems to have bought me a lifetime membership in the crisis counseling club. Which brings me to my current situation.

I am part of the late Mrs. Freison's caseload. She isn't dead. More likely just resting. Mrs. Freison, inconsiderately for the purposes of building my self-esteem, cracked up during one of my sessions. That's not as significant as it sounds. She was never very stable. She had left her husband and kids and moved to Smithers to be with a guy half her age who lived on top of his parents' garage, and after he left her for an eighteen-year-old gas station attendant at Petrocan, she was never the same.

It's a good thing I am very open-minded and tolerant about mental illness, because if I wasn't, I would have been offended by Mrs. Freison's parting remarks. And even though she was shaking and crying when she told me I had an almost "freakish ability to see things the wrong way, coupled with a shocking poverty of age-appropriate real-life experience," I was still a bit hurt. Then she said, chest heaving with sobs, hands full of hair, that from what she'd seen over our endless four years together, my ten-year-old brother, MacGregor, had far more maturity than I was ever likely to have. She accused me of hiding from life in books and harboring strange obsessions and staying at home all the time to torture my poor parents, who are the only people who can't legally get away from me.

Nice, eh?

"Insight is cheap, Alice. Especially warped insight. And that's the only kind you have." Sob, sob, sob.

Then Mrs. Freison said *she* was getting away, in a body bag if she had to, but she was getting away. Then the paramedics came.

I may have opened up a bit too much with Mrs. Freison. In fact, I was just telling her about how the dangers of peer interactions are illustrated in the group behavior of chickens (based on my observations of our neighbors' hobby-farm poultry). I described how chickens choose one outcast to peck, and the only way to protect the unlucky one is to cover it with tar or maybe homeschool it. I thought it was a pretty convincing argument, but Mrs. F. sort of screamed and said that chickens didn't have peers. People had peers and they weren't that bad. Anyway, I refuse to take responsibility for her meltdown. I don't see myself as counselor burnout material. Maybe that bald girl with the big boots who hangs around here. Now *she* looks troubled.

I get counseled at the Teens in Transition (Not in Trouble) Club. It's supposed to be a haven for those of us suffering from "adjustment difficulties." They've tried to fool us into thinking that the club's a regular teen hangout by putting in a Ping-Pong table, but the Single Mother Spot with its Learn to Cook and Clean area and the Feelings Room, painted blue-black in a lame effort to be hip and sympathetic, are dead giveaways. The place is also lousy with helping professionals: social workers, parole officers, and of course the on-staff counselor.

They've hired a new counselor to replace Mrs. Freison. The rumor is that the new one's just a trainee. I don't know if a novice is really the right person for this job. After all, the clients are messed up enough to willingly walk into a place that has the words TROUBLE and TEEN written in two-foot-high letters on its plywood sign out front. I had a fully trained, very experienced professional, and look what happened to her. And I'm pretty much a poster child for mental health compared to some of the kids in this place.

There were three of us waiting to see the new guy this afternoon, and I'm proud to say I was easily the least messed up. The girl to the right of me cried the whole time. After listening to her for almost fifteen minutes, I finally felt I had to say something.

"Uh, is anything wrong?"

"No," the girl moaned, and swiped at her eyes with her sleeve.

The girl sitting on the other side of me snorted and said, "So why don't you shut the hell up, then? You're driving me crazy."

The weeper didn't stop but shifted to silent crying.

One of the single mothers/peer counselors must have overheard the exchange, because she was over like a shot.

"Can't you see she's upset? That's not how we talk to each other in here."

Encouraged, the weeper turned up the volume slightly.

Sour Girl turned to Single Mother Girl. "If you weren't holding that kid, I'd show you how I talk to people—"

"Oh yeah?" demanded Single Mother Girl, looking around for somewhere to stash her baby.

Just then the door to the counselor's office swung open and the new counselor poked his head out.

We all turned to look at him.

"Hi," he whispered throatily.

Three mouths dropped open. Mine had the dignity to stay closed. All ceased.

"Hi," the other girls answered in hypnotized unity.

It was like a snake charmer had just started a good song.

Weepy Girl went in for her appointment, and former enemies Sour and Single went into action with their compacts and hairbrushes, giggling and using the word *cute* over and over.

The whole thing was sort of interesting because I've been going to the club for a long time now and that's about the most civilized interaction I've seen.

Oh God, it's almost my turn to meet the new guy. This should be rewarding. Maybe even a turning point.

Later

The bad news is that my new counselor seems at least as troubled as the old one. I mean, he seems basically nice and everything, but he's obviously riddled with issues. Low self-esteem, unresolved family-of-origin issues, boundary problems—Death Lord Bob has them all.

His name is actually Bob, or Robert, I guess, but he looks like a Death Lord to me. He has a small goatee, dresses in black from head to toe, wears a turtleneck and waistcoat, and carries a black leather briefcase that looks like a medical bag. The bag is filled with his counselor textbooks and copies of *A Course in Miracles* and other self-help books. But it looks like it should be filled with equipment of doom and destruction—you know, neutralizers and death scepters and stuff.

I'm not one to brag, but frankly I think Bob got more out of that session than I did. In this hushed, just-between-you-and-me voice, he told me about how his childhood was quite bad and everything, and how being back in a small town like Smithers for his practicum was "bringing up a lot of issues" related to his own small-town upbringing. Apparently his complaining is some kind of technique to get me to feel comfortable enough to open up and "share where I'm at" with him. So far it's not working.

I realize Bob needs to learn and everything, and I don't mind helping out. But I have to say that I'm glad my psychological well-being isn't, like, dependent on our appointments. The session only really helped by making me feel relieved that at least I'm not as screwed up as he is.

July 18
Today Death Lord Bob informed me that I need to decide what I want out of therapy. He's very pushy and results-oriented in some ways, even though he whispers. I wonder if he went to business school before deciding to become a helping professional.

One interesting thing about Bob is that his voice doesn't really fit his personality. You would think that some guy whispering about his abandonment issues would sound wimpy. But Death Lord sounds like Clint Eastwood talking tough to the warden or something. He probably has the most masculine whisper I've ever heard. That must be what's got all the new Teens in Transition hanging around. Before Bob came, there were about ten helping professionals for every troubled teen. Now the place seems packed with maladjusted young people. And it's not just teenagers jostling for position outside Bob's door either. I'm guessing the off-duty social workers hovering around lately aren't here to do a little extra helping and nurturing. They sure weren't anywhere to be found when Mrs. F. was up against the ropes. Emotionally speaking.

I told Bob that I don't have any goals for therapy because it was my parents' idea to help offset any problems related to my lack of peer interaction. They enrolled me in counseling after that Home-Based Learners' Picnic we went to a few years ago. It was supposed to be an opportunity to "socialize with other home-based learners in a noncoercive atmosphere."

My parents looked around and realized that the home-schooled kids weren't exactly what my dad called "paragons of normalcy." A disturbing number of them were still breast-feeding at an age when most kids are taking up smoking. One boy wore antlers all afternoon. His sister's eyes rolled around in her head when she sang the Appalachian folk songs her mother insisted she perform for us in preparation for her big debut on the summer folk-music festival circuit. Those kids were called Fleet and Arrow, so they really never had a chance. Fleet's parents didn't tell her that her lotto-machine eye action looked weird because they didn't want to damage her self-esteem.

I thought it was sort of my duty to give Fleet some honest feedback, so I told her that when she sang, she looked a bit like Linda Blair in *The Exorcist*, which I'd seen at my cousin's house. That led to Fleet's mother having to tell her about the existence of Catholicism, which made her mother so angry that she told my parents I would not be welcome at their yurt for the May Day Festival.

But Fleet and Arrow were practically normal compared to the religious homeschooled kids. At that same picnic one of the religious parents told my mother I was a demon spawn after I told her daughter that girls were allowed to wear pants.

That was the end of my parents' attempts to get me to socialize with other housebound kids. It was just as well, because my mom was starting to get pressure to declare whether her noncurriculum was unschooling, deschooling, or homeschooling. There's a lot of friction between the different factions, and Mom didn't want to end up in the wrong camp.

The reality is that what I've been doing is self-schooling. Sure, my mom and dad take turns pretending to teach me. My mom specializes in giving me alternative family books in which everyone is gay, as well as environmental books like *Silent Spring*, which haven't exactly helped to make me into a sunny optimist. Dad takes the afternoon shift and supposedly teaches me science and math, although mostly what we do is drink coffee and read *Popular Science* and

Omni and other books and magazines. Sometimes, when he's feeling guilty, he makes me do the math sheets he borrowed from another homeschooling parent, but those lessons grind to a halt whenever I have a question.

But Bob seems unwilling to consider the emotional and intellectual handicaps I have from my homeschooling history. He said he knew that counseling wasn't my idea, but we might as well make the best of it. At the end of today's groundbreaking session he whispered moodily that for next time he's looking forward to talking over my therapeutic goals. For the past four years I have successfully avoided participating in my counseling sessions, so this turn of events is a bit of a blow.

Later

I've been giving it a lot of thought, and I've decided that maybe the helping professionals are right. Maybe I haven't seen enough of life. Maybe I'm not growing enough, or in the right areas. I'm not one to take on a challenge, but it could be that my life could use some direction. But I don't need goals for therapy. What I need is goals for my life. So that's what I'm going to get.

LIFE GOALS LIST

1. Decide on a unique and innovative career path (to get helping professionals off my back).
1a. Get part-time job in preparation for said career path?

Too much like work? (Should be outside family home.)

2. Increase contact with people outside of immediate family. (Not friends, necessarily, but at least superficial interaction of the "Hi, how are you?" variety with people who are not home-based learners and who do not attend the Teens in Transition Club.)

3. Learn to drive a car (but not our car, because I do have my nonexistent reputation to consider).

4. Some sort of boy-girl interaction? (Possibly best left until after high school. Maybe best left until middle age.)

5. Publish paper comparing teenagers and chicken peer groups (in LANCET or other respected publication?).

6. Read entire LORD OF THE RINGS series to prove that early, parent-assisted reading of THE HOBBIT was not just an aberration, and I really am advanced for my age. (Do not dress like the characters.)

There. I'm sure I can achieve those things. I can probably even get through the big ones by the end of the summer. I've moved my dad's *Lord of the Rings* boxed set into my room in preparation for some mature reading.

Ten Minutes Later
I am pleased to report that I am making rapid progress on

my Life Goals. Bob is a genius. Career ideas are coming in fast and furious. I was directionless ten minutes ago, but now, thanks to my new Life Goals and an article on the Ukraine I read in *National Geographic*, I have realized that it is my calling to be an Easter-egg painter. I'll paint tiny religious scenes on eggs. I can't believe I didn't think of this sooner. It was a serious oversight on the part of the Home Learners' Career Planning pamphlet to forget to include Easter-egg painter in the list of possible vocations. Nurse, doctor, lawyer, secretary, egg iconography painter. Maybe I could paint famous people on the eggs when there is no religious holiday to celebrate. I could do Elvis eggs, rock star eggs, you name it. On second thought, it's probably better to stick with the religious pictures; they are more traditional and there's always a market for them.

Twenty Minutes Later
Maybe careers aren't something you can really plan for. They just sort of happen, like brown eyes or flat feet. I took one of those career aptitude tests last year, and it showed that I should be a flight attendant or a seamstress. Not a fashion designer or anything, mind you, but a sweatshop worker. Apparently stewardesses and sweatshop workers and I enjoy a lot of the same interests and activities.

When I pointed out to my mom that I'm afraid to fly and can't sew, and besides, the garment district in Smithers consists only of Herringbone and Heather Menswear and Northlight Jeans Fashion Emporium and

Bridal Outlet, so there really isn't anywhere to practice my sweatshop laborer trade, she accused me of being negative and closed-minded. No argument there. Although it seems to me that if ninety percent of the adults I know, including my parents, don't know what they want to be when they grow up, it's a bit much to ask of me, at the tender age of fifteen.

Maybe I should pick some careers out of a hat and just start doing them. I know I can't just drop in and start doing surgery on someone, but I could be one of those people who hang around the fringes of a profession or industry, hoping to be mistaken for someone who belongs. I could get a white coat and hang out in the pharmacy part of the drugstore reorganizing the vitamin B section like I really know what I am doing. Or I could act really official in the video store and give my opinion to customers with ringing authority.

It's too bad that the nearest lighthouse is in Prince Rupert, which is at least a seven-hour drive away from Smithers. For a really good people-free profession I think lighthouse keeper would be outstanding.

Or, if I'm looking for isolation, I could just hang around the night shift at the mill. I could make myself useful by ratting out the graveyard-shift guys who sit in their trucks on their lunch breaks using those little blowtorches to smoke hash.

I wonder if my history as a homeschooled child might be a career obstacle, maybe even a Life Goal impediment?

AS FOR ME AND MY LIFE GOALS

July 19
A new day, a new Life Goal.

Life Goal No. 7: Develop new look. (Like career
choice, must reflect uniqueness).

Today I was mistaken for a salesperson at the
Workwear Well. I wasn't even trying to pass, either. Some
woman came up to me and asked where she might find the
Stanfield long underwear in red. She seemed a bit dimwitted.
She realized her mistake after I shot her my best look of
loathing. Then she sort of cackled and said she couldn't tell
one kid from another. What that meant I can't even begin
to guess. It's disturbing to me that I bear the stamp of
Workwear's so strongly.

I know I don't want to be a fashion designer or model
or anything, but I also know I don't want to look like a
poster child for the working classes. So far I've tried to
avoid the fashion thing altogether. My standard uniform is
jeans and a plaid shirt. I can see that if I'm going to establish any kind of individual identity, it's going to have to be
reflected in my clothes.

I think I'll take my style cues from my cousin Frank

(that's actually her name—her parents were very active in the drug culture of the sixties). She has a lot of style. I remember my dad saying when we were younger that he could have paid off our mortgage with the money from one of Frank's outfits. I hadn't seen her for a few years, but when she came to visit us earlier this spring, she looked as good as ever. I could tell right off that she has an alternative value system. Her hair was short and waved back, like hair from the twenties. Her eyebrows were thin and arched. She wore a green-and-blue down-filled vest and red polyester stretch pants with silver platform shoes. The effect was very, well, alternative.

Frank was supposed to stay for a week while she waited to get in to see a doctor in Vancouver for some special kind of treatment. I was dying to talk to her, but she only came out of her room to go to the bathroom. She must have a small bladder or something, because she seemed to have to go about every ten minutes.

By noon I'd seen most of Frank's outfits. She wore eight different ones before lunch. Her fourth ensemble included a curly gray wig and a tiara. At one point she stopped giggling for a minute and came into the kitchen and sang "Ave Maria." Then she changed into some knee-high boots and did a number called "These Boots Are Made for Walking." I really liked it, but Dad didn't seem impressed. Around the sixth outfit, before she went outside to chase the neighbors' chickens around, I got over my intimidation and told Frank I was interested in looking more like her. She said all I needed was a few more barrettes. She went back into the guest room and came out with a handful. Most were little metal clips, but some were plastic ones like the ones little kids wear. Frank put them all over my head.

It wasn't quite the look I was after. She clipped too many on one side, so I was a dead ringer for that pinhead guy in the horror movies. When Mom saw me, she said early-onset dementia wasn't my look. She can be incredibly tasteless and insensitive at times.

Before I could get any more advice, Frank disappeared. She used the pellet gun to help round up the neighbors' chickens, and they (the neighbors, not the chickens) complained to my parents. My mother panicked and called the hospital to ask if Frank's behavior was "normal for a girl in her condition." The hospital said they had no idea and suggested that Mom call the police if her niece was menacing domestic livestock with a gun. Personally, I think the incident serves the Stankes right for keeping a so-called hobby farm within the town limits. It makes the whole neighborhood look a bit too agricultural, if you know what I mean. That is something we should really be trying to move away from. Anyway, Mom and Dad had a debate about whether calling the police wasn't a little extreme; after all, it wasn't like Frank had been waving the .22 around. Frank must have heard them, because she was gone when they went to check her room. We found out later that she hitchhiked back to Vancouver, where she moved in with a boy named Glue.

Frank's little visit upset my mother, but my dad told

her it was unrealistic to think that coming to Smithers would help set anyone on the road to sobriety. He said it was more likely to make someone recognize the important role drugs play in making life bearable. Mom didn't want to tell her brother, Uncle Laird, that we'd lost Frank. Uncle Laird is a rich lawyer, and he has always given Frank the best of everything. According to Dad, Frank's last treatment center cost $15,000 a month. Frank has this great satin bomber jacket with the words BETTY FORD printed on the back. I hope it was included in the price. In the end Uncle Laird didn't end up reacting all that badly to the news of Frank's disappearance. Mom said it was almost like he was expecting it.

The thing I found fascinating was how Frank, who is apparently a drug addict, could fit so many clothes into a Barbie lunch bucket and Brady Bunch knapsack.

Anyway, this latest assault on my dignity at the Workwear Well has cemented my commitment to follow Frank's fashion lead. I think I need a haircut. A trip to the New in View thrift store may also be in order. But I'm a bit worried that, with everyone in this town fixated on the stinky sixties, the New in View people won't have kept the stuff from the seventies. I read magazines. I know what's hot and what's not.

For lack of anything else to say at my last appointment, I told Death Lord about Frank's visit and how I'm working on some Life Goals but I'm not ready to talk about them yet. I think he felt like we were making major progress. He said that it's important to talk about the dysfunction in our families of origin if we are ever to work out a new dynamic for our interpersonal interfacing. Yeah, thanks, Bob.

July 20

I've finally hit upon a good career. I think I will be a cultural critic. I bet the criticizing profession will make good use of all my malcontent feelings and total negativity. In fact, these might be prerequisites. I got the idea from this magazine article I was reading. The writer was a very important cultural critic, and he certainly had nothing positive to say. Like me, he seemed to feel that the state of the world is appalling. Living in Smithers and being a homeschooled shut-in may even be an asset for a cultural critic.

I think I'll be a radical but well-respected critic, possibly involved with things like performance art involving real blood, but not the sensationalistic kind. My art will be serious commentary. I'll be quite angry and my writings will be sharp-edged satire—like that *Rape of the Lock* I read last year. Classic writings.

I find I have a natural tendency for critical thinking. Like a few years ago, when my parents tried to get me to call them by their first names: Diane and John. They thought it would help us to have a less hierarchical relationship. They seemed to think I would feel like it was a big honor to call them by their first names. I gave the issue some critical thought and decided it was an inappropriate attempt on their part to abdicate parental responsibilities, possibly connected to a pathetic and unhealthy refusal to admit their true age. I mean, they *are* getting on. So I decided to call them Mom and Dad until I'm in my late forties to help with role reinforcement and age-appropriate behavior. I even tried Mommy and Daddy for a while, but it was too much, even for me. Mother and Father is okay, but used exclusively makes me sound sort of stuck-up. So I call them Mom and Dad as much as possible, especially in public. There's no mistaking us for some unusually progressive family if I'm calling them Mom and Dad. Now if that doesn't show critical reasoning on my part, I don't know what would. I guess I just have a knack.

Later

Since deciding to become a cultural critic, I find I have become quite critical. My dad says that is a far cry from becoming discerning, but he doesn't know anything. God, I mean he's never even read *Spin* magazine. He keeps trying to tell me that *Rolling Stone* was his generation's *Spin*. Yeah, right.

I probably shouldn't have informed my parents of my new potential career path. After all, they are my parents, and it's more or less my duty to keep things of a personal nature from them. In my own defense, I didn't exactly *tell* them. I told MacGregor and they overheard. MacGregor is my brother, and even though he's only ten years old, he's a very good listener and has a lot of integrity. He's into nature but not in a posing-for-candid-shots, protest-poster, hippie kind of way. Instead, he's always wandering around looking at bugs and rooting around in swamps and ponds. He subscribes to *Owl* magazine. MacGregor is the kind of person who could wear an unmatched pair of gum boots all day and never notice. I think MacGregor might be a genius. Anyone so oblivious to the horror of the human world must be.

My parents tried to homeschool MacGregor, but he was too advanced for them. Plus he seems to have no problem getting along in a regular classroom setting. He's quite an inspiration to me. I told him about my cultural criticism plans this afternoon while he worked on his tanks. He keeps tropical fish, but only the "sustainable kind" that breed in captivity. He is trying to get his angelfish to have babies and is rearranging the tank furniture to get the mood just right. How he knows what kind of romantic setting fish want is just one of the many amazing things about my younger brother.

I suggested he move the piece of driftwood a couple of inches to the left for maximum sex action and he just laughed.

Oh well, it's nearly time for dinner, and we have company. My mom's friend Geraldine and her daughter, Jane, stopped in "for a minute" over an hour ago. Geraldine's not one to leave if a meal's being served. My mom met her at some home-based educators' conference on dealing with difficult teens, and they immediately hit it off. Thank God they've given up on trying to make Jane and me friends. For one thing, Jane is about ten years older than me. And for another, she's pretty angry. She changed her name from Cheyenne Summer to Jane, and even if I don't like her all that much, I approve of that. Jane still lives at home and her mom says she's working on her tenth grade certificate. For some reason Jane and her mother go almost everywhere together, but Jane never gets out of the car. She sits inside it smoking and reading and scowling.

When they come over, my mom makes a point of going outside and asking Jane to come inside, but she always refuses. One time I went out and asked her if she wanted to come in. She looked up from her book, pulled her glasses down her nose with one finger, blew a stream of smoke out her nose, and said, "You're aware that you're doomed, eh?"

Now I let my mom do the inviting.

It's understandable that Jane's temperament is a bit dark. Her mother's awful. The only cool thing about Geraldine is that she looks like James Woods. What is it with my mother and these sad, messy old hippie chicks? My first target as a cultural critic will be people who never got over the sixties!

July 21

I went to see a movie last night with my dad and MacGregor. It was really great. It was quite serious but funny and it was low budget. It was so good, it had musicians acting in it, and it won some prizes in Europe and everything. I'm thinking of doing an in-depth cultural criticism of it. You know, I could talk about its implications for our culture or something. The criticism wouldn't be very biting or scathing, though, since the movie was really good.

We went to the movies because Dad wanted to avoid at least part of Geraldine's visit. As usual, she accepted the invitation to stay for dinner, even though Jane had already been waiting out in the car for over an hour. Dad's not too crazy about Geraldine. He doesn't go in for what he calls "all that laziness masquerading as counter-culture." Actually, Dad doesn't go in for much, but he keeps pretty busy doing it. He complains that Geraldine smells like dope all the time. Mom says it's just her per-fume. I think it might have something to do with Jane's smoking. Sometimes you can hardly see her in the car, the haze is so thick. Who knows what she's smoking in there? Considering her parentage, anything is possible.

On the personal development front, I have begun reading *The Fellowship of the Ring*, which is the first book in the *Lord of the Rings* trilogy. It's the kind of thing that every cultural critic should read. We are often more interested in science fiction and fantasy than aver-age people. I'm on page two and really enjoying it. So far I like it just as much as I did *The Hobbit*, which really says something about me, I think.

July 25

Today Death Lord Bob wanted to hear more about my Life Goals. For some reason I felt compelled to lie to him. I told him that my goal was to go back to regular school! I have no idea why I told him that. I guess I just felt like he was looking for something a little more substantial than reading a few books. Unfortunately, Bob took it quite seriously. He got all excited and said how honored he was to have been "a real catalyst for change" in my life, and he was so glad he chose to go into counseling as a profession and "days like this make it all worthwhile." He was practically jumping up and down. He said he's going to do everything in his power to make sure the "transition is smooth" and assured me that "we are going to make this journey together."

What have I done? How am I going to tell my parents?

Later

I didn't have to tell my parents. Bob did. And here's the incredible thing. They think it's a great idea. You'd almost think they didn't want to homeschool me anymore.

My mom said it's natural for me to move back into the world. My dad said graduating with a proper high school diploma will "open a lot of doors for me."

I don't think I'm ready for school. My only confidence comes from MacGregor. He said he knows I can do it. I hope he's right.

July 28

Bob doesn't waste any time. He's got me enrolled already! Well, almost. He spoke to the counselor, and they decided that based on my special background and unusual circumstances, I am going to have to go to the Alternative Solutions School rather than the regular high school.

According to the brochure Bob gave me, the Alternative has a "partnering relationship" with the Teens in Transition Club. The two "solutions-based institutions" are supposed to "offer young people a seamless support network for growing." When I showed my dad, he said that what they definitely offer is an "absolute flair for acronyms," whatever that means. Bob arranged for me to take English in the regular high school, because I am supposedly advanced in that area, but my important classes, like Life Skills and Family Studies, will be in the Alternative. He told me that the other Alternative students are an eclectic mix. I asked what that meant, and he hemmed and hawed and said that all the students are special in different ways. Some are there because they are top-level athletes and have to travel a lot and need a flexible schedule. Others have talents that need special nurturing. Maybe my advanced vocabulary is going to be my special talent. I can't decide whether I'm excited about going to the Alternative or disappointed. It should be interesting meeting all those athletes, though. Maybe I'll be inspired to take up a sport other than reading and criticizing.

HELMET HEAD

August 2

A mother-daughter shopping trip shouldn't cause post-traumatic stress disorder, should it? Well, in my family any outing is cause for concern.

My mother and I went shopping and got my hair done today. Mom dropped me at the New in View thrift store to find some cool, Frank-like clothes while she went to the health food store. I was amazed at how much macramé the New in View had. My mom has a couple of plant hangers made out of the stuff that are older than me. It must be indestructible. I could have bought a whole macramé outfit—vest, bell bottoms, hat, purse, and Bible cover—but decided against it. I figured it probably wouldn't help my mood any to dress in a material that feels so much like hay.

The New in View was a little short on what my *Complete Guide to Thrifting* book calls "scores." The stuff was cheap but not very cool. The Zellers and Fields tags were still on all the stretch pants. I found a pair of red-and-blue-checked four-way stretch pants and an orange tank top from the kids' bin. The store didn't have many down-filled vests, but I finally found a green one that must have belonged to a very small logger. It looks a bit like a life preserver, but it was the best I could do. I also got some nursing shoes. They didn't have any of those cool striped sneakers from the seventies, but I figured I could draw some stripes on the nurse shoes at home.

After I finished shopping at the New in View, Mom and I went over to Irma's Salon to get my hair trimmed so it would look better in barrettes. Irma's been giving me the Special ever since my mom retired the bowl. Irma has only one haircut, and she gives it to every single customer. But this time I told Irma I was after something a little different. I wanted my hair to look old-fashioned, big toward the back, and really short, just like Frank's. Irma acted like she knew exactly what I wanted, like she did alternative haircuts all the time. At first she and my mom were so busy talking that she didn't even seem to be looking at what she was doing. Then Mom went over to the Grocery Giant to finish her shopping, and for about five minutes Irma made a big show of getting into my haircut. If a furrowed brow and look of extreme concentration meant a good haircut, I would have the best in town. She moved from side to side, snipping here and there, and pursing her lips. I was starting to feel sick from all her ducking and weaving around my head. Irma's probably too old to move so quickly, and I was almost grateful when another customer came in and Irma went back to gossiping and barely looking at what she was doing to my head.

The whole thing was beginning to scare me. I couldn't see how the mess Irma was making on my head would ever look like the hair on those girls who hang out at raves or whatever those big dances are called. Finally Irma got out the blow-dryer and a big round brush shaped like a curler. She said that the brush was the key to getting the old-fashioned look. By then I had my eyes squeezed shut. I opened them again when my mom came in and said "Oh" in this strange way.

My hair was huge. I don't know what Irma did, but my flat, straight hair was the size and shape of a construction helmet. The big part, which was supposed to be at the back of my head, was actually right on top, and my bangs plunged daringly toward my right eyebrow. When my mom pointed out how uneven my bangs were, Irma made a little stab at straightening them, but even I could see that too much adjustment would make me bald on my forehead. It was like when I tried trimming Barbie's hair and in trying to get her hair even ended up leaving her with only little plugs of plastic bristles coming out of her scalp.

My mom was totally upset. She actually said, "My God, Irma. I don't even know if I should pay for this. It looks absolutely bizarre."

Irma got defensive and said it was what I had asked for.

It was bad enough that I looked like a monster, but a fight between my mother and the most spiteful, gossipy hairdresser in town was more than I could handle. Everybody who complained about an Irma haircut was later heard to be a lesbian, or an infidel who cheated on her husband.

I went and sat in the car while they worked it out. We have an ocean liner of an automobile with fins and everything. It might actually be sort of cool if it wasn't rusted and covered with stickers for every lame folk band that has ever come through town. My mom and all her Folk Music Society friends are always getting really excited about some band of middle-aged ladies getting in touch with themselves through second careers in music and singing about menopause and other things that no one really wants to hear about. And then there are the exploited children of folk music, like Fleet and Arrow, to consider. The audience and the performers all wear way too much purple, if you ask me.

Sitting out there with my football head in the parking lot of the Smithers Shopping Center, I was feeling pretty low, even with my new cool clothes. I was trying to calculate how many barrettes it would take to weigh down the lump on my head, and whether it would be grown out by the time school started, when someone knocked on the car window. Embarrassed, I tried to pretend I didn't hear. I stared straight ahead with a mean look on my face, but the knocking continued. When I looked up, I knew I was in hell.

Two boys were staring in at me. And standing with them was the dread blond menace of first grade: Linda. My heart gave a thud and then began to jackhammer.

I hadn't seen Linda for years. She didn't look as though she'd mellowed any.

I glanced at the three of them out of the corner of my eye, hoping they would just go away. The dark-haired boy in the Whitesnake T-shirt knocked on the window again, and I looked up and smiled weakly.

31

Whitesnake Boy told me to roll down the window. I didn't want to seem scared, so I did. He asked what happened to my hair. The blond boy in the Judas Priest T-shirt said it looked like somebody'd put my head in a wood chipper. Linda just smirked.

"Jack, ask her why she won't answer us," demanded the dark-haired boy.

"Why won't you answer Kevin?" asked the obedient Jack.

They reached their hands in through the open window, trying to touch my huge hair.

"Aaagh," said Kevin, "my hand's stuck." He'd put his fingers through the shell of Aqua Net into the rat's nest of tangles Irma had back-combed underneath for volume.

Just then my mom came charging out of the salon. She took one look at Linda in her acid-wash jeans and the boys in their heavy-metal T-shirts, grabbing at my hair through the windows of the Wonderwagon, and went ballistic.

She stormed over, a whirlwind in purple and pink cotton, tie-dyed scarves flying every which way.

"Hey! Hey!"

She was moving into her truly pissed shriek. I couldn't believe it. There I was, trapped in the rust wagon with monster hair, and my hippie freak mother was about to do battle with the local head bangers.

Mom started yelling, "Are you touching my daughter's hair? Are you touching her hair? You had better not be putting your low-rent hands on my daughter's hair!"

She sounded like that guy in *Taxi Driver*, only even more psycho.

Jack looked at Kevin and backed away from my mother. "She's wiggin', man," he said. "Hey, we weren't doing nothin'."

Then Linda brilliantly told my enraged mother that not only was I dead meat, but she (my mom) was a bitch. My mother, whose grip on herself isn't the tightest at the best of times, got even louder. She started screaming at Linda about sociopaths and pacifism. It was a pretty incoherent performance, even for her.

I took the opportunity to roll up my window.

People started to come out of the shopping center to stare blankly at my hysterical mother. Linda coiled up, and before I knew it, she moved in and slapped my mom, hard. Then she sprang back, arms open at her sides, hands in loose fists, like some kind of martial arts fighter.

Mom stood still for a moment. I don't think Kevin and Jack were even breathing at this point. Then my mother launched herself at Linda, grabbed her by the lapels of her jean jacket, and threw her on the ground. On the ground, if you can believe it! Linda kicked viciously until she knocked my mother down with her. They pummeled each other like a couple of kindergartners in a fight over who gets to eat the Play-Doh, only it wasn't children, it was my pink-and-purple mother and the worst girl in town rolling around in the parking lot of the Smithers Grocery Giant.

I had this moment where I could see it all from outside. Me and my hair in the vast, finned station wagon staring out like a caged alien at a forty-year-old woman in hippie garb in a catfight with a small, blond-feathered head-banger girl. It was a defining moment, the kind you worry about in those nights where you can't sleep, the kind that can ruin any hopes a person might have of a normal life.

Anyway, Mr. Scott, who works in produce, and Ralph from canned goods broke it up. Mr. Scott waded in and lifted my mother off Linda. Mom immediately burst into tears. Ralph caught Linda as she tried to go after Mom again, and Linda bit Ralph's hand right to the bone. He needed five stitches to close it up. Some bag boys came to Ralph's assistance, and together they held Linda, who, by this time, was grunting and snarling and spitting like an animal.

When the Royal Canadian Mounted Police showed up, my mom was still crying and Mr. Scott was awkwardly patting her on the back and looking embarrassed, yet manly and concerned. Jack and Kevin had disappeared. Linda was surrounded by a collection of hyper bag boys, and Ralph, white as a ghost, was being tended to by a group of checkout girls. Me and my hair were still sitting in the car with the windows rolled up.

With the entire Grocery Giant staff giving assistance, I really didn't think there was much I could do. After all, they're trained to help.

The police officer spoke to a couple of people. When

he approached Linda and she called him an "f–ing pig," his eyebrows rose slowly and he moved in a little closer to her.

In a quiet counselor-to-mental patient voice, he asked Linda what was going on, and all the bag boys started talking at once. He listened, nodded, and then asked her again what happened. When she tried to kick him, he sighed and said, "Okay, Linda. If that's how you want it."

Then he picked her up, screaming, yelling, and kicking, and put her in the prisoner part of the cruiser. After he locked her in, you could see her enraged face screaming silently. Then her head disappeared, and her feet, with only one high-top sneaker on, appeared and began smashing at the windows, hard enough to make the car shake.

The officer took notes while he talked to my sobbing mother and the gray-faced and bleeding Ralph. Kevin and Jack were nowhere to be seen. When the cop knocked on my window, I rolled it down, looking, I hoped, innocent of any involvement.

"Can you tell me what happened here, Miss?"

"Oh. Um. Hard to say, really."

"Well, is that your mother over there?" he asked, pointing to my tear-stained mother, who stared at me with this horrified look.

"Oh. Her. Well, yes. I guess so."

"Look, young lady," he said. "Maybe you should tell me what went on here. You know, your mother is pretty upset. Does this have anything to do with your hair?"

I gave him the whole story, helped along by my mother's indignant promptings.

"I can't believe you! These kids were attacking you! Of course you know who they are!"

She obviously didn't remember Linda from my brief school career.

"You saw that girl attack me. You were right there in the car."

She turned pathetically to the officer. "You have to understand, officer, after what Irma did to her hair . . ."

Apparently Officer Ross felt quite sorry for my mother having to deal with me, so he sent us home and asked Mom to decide whether she wanted to press charges against Linda. Ralph was adamant that Linda was too crazy for him to consider charges. He said he would never be able to relax in the parking lot again if he thought she might be after him.

That was our mother-daughter Saturday at the mall. I have to go to bed now due to exhaustion at reliving the trauma. My parents have decided that my behavior was unnatural. Even my dad said that it was completely unacceptable to sit in the car with the windows rolled up while my mother was attacked by "marauding white trash."

Before she stopped speaking to me, my mother asked me if I thought she should press charges. I said something along the lines of "Oh, that will really make my life fun when I try and go back to school." She asked me what I thought we should do, and I told her I'd like to forget the whole embarrassing incident. She said she was just trying to protect me, and I said why didn't she just kill me and get it over with. Then she cried and told my dad she couldn't take it anymore. Shades of Mrs. Freison, if you ask me. Next thing you know *she'll* be after the boy down at the Shell station.

Whatever.

It strikes me that perhaps what I learned today is that I would be a good observer of some kind. You know, one of those people who watch things happen and don't feel the need to get involved. What are they called? Oh yeah, impartial observers. They go to wars and demonstrations and things and just watch. I could be quite good at that. I'm already in the late stages of advanced detachment where my mother is concerned. With a little practice I could feel that way about everyone.

August 3

I spent all morning trying out my new look. It certainly is radical.

Colorwise, at least, I think I look pretty good in my orange tank top and red-and-blue-checked stretch pants. The green vest would probably look better over a turtle-neck or at least something with sleeves, but I want to wear as much of my new stuff as possible.

My hair still looks really bad. I washed it and let it dry naturally, but it is still lumpy and uneven. There are huge chunks missing here and there that just look like mistakes instead of the radical hairdo I was hoping for. I would like to get my hair fixed, but I would have to get my head shaved to even it out.

I tried wearing barrettes at the front like Frank, but

there really isn't enough hair to hold them properly, so I put a few clips on the lump at the top of my head to try to hold it down. Maybe I would look better with my eyebrows plucked all thin and arched like Frank's. I won't get Irma to do it, though. She'd have me looking like an especially ugly extra on *Star Trek*.

My parents still aren't speaking to me. Dad stared at me hard when he saw my new look, but he turned away fast and didn't say anything.

Mom isn't looking too great today either. She has a black eye and a couple of big scratches on her face. To be honest, she looks sort of tacky. She has been deep into her granola routine—meditating, playing sucky New Age music, and drinking gallons of Wandering Serenity tea in between phone calls to all her friends, telling them what happened. I expect the bean casseroles to start pouring in any minute to help her get through this time of trouble. I overheard her telling one that she's decided not to press charges because there might be "repercussions" and the "authorities don't seem to be able to do anything about the level of violence in this town." You'd think she was Gandhi, rather than practically the instigator of the whole thing.

I don't think she's telling them too much about my part in the Battle at High Noon. She's got this competitive thing about her family. I know she wants to be able to brag about me, but so far there hasn't really been anything to brag about other than the fact that I rarely leave the house. She's too proud to admit that she envies her friends whose children have friends, work at food co-ops, belong to Greenpeace, and attend regular school.

Mom sometimes talks about my independence and nonconformity like they are good things, but I know that a pessimistic, bitter misfit isn't at all what she had in mind when she took it upon herself to conceive her first-born, even if that child is quite advanced in some areas, such as irony and vocabulary. Oh well, maybe Death Lord will have better luck than Mrs. F. in turning me into the person my mother wants me to be.

Dad is a bit more real. He's not much of a people person, but he's so good-looking it doesn't matter. He's also pretty smart, but not in any useful way, as Grandma likes to point out. He spends quite a lot of time in the basement writing what he calls "bodice rippers." Mom suspects that it's pornography and is always checking to make sure his stories aren't degrading women. Dad hasn't actually had anything published yet, so the soft porn/romance novel thing isn't exactly a big money-maker. He only turns out about one little story every three or four months, and they are very historical and have a lot of women whose dresses are so tight, they are always fainting into "dead swoons." Apparently the market for that sort of thing is limited. He is still con-vinced that he is going to make a fortune as a writer and is continually referring to his copy of *Making It Writing Romance* for inspiration.

He is also good at titles. He keeps a binder full of them. *The President's Neck Is Missing: A Rex E. Fortescue*

Mystery is one of my personal favorites. If he had a book to go with it, I think it could have real potential.

Dad has had quite a few careers. He has done just about everything that a person can do without a lot of preparation. Unfortunately, he gets tired of his careers quickly. When he was younger, he was a musician and played guitar. That's what he was doing when he met my mom. She says she fell in love with him because she couldn't resist a man with a guitar. That brings up all sorts of embarrassing my-mother-the-groupie scenarios. I try not to think about it. Anyway, Dad's not a musician anymore because he finds it "soul killing" to cover other people's songs. I suppose I can see his point. Having the local crowd call for "Stairway to Heaven" every five minutes would be enough to kill anyone's love for music. On the other hand, I don't think Dad exactly worked himself to death writing new material, so playing covers was really his only option.

Dad would probably be sort of disappointing to my mother, too, if he wasn't so good-looking and such a magnet to the folk festival babes, especially the ones who are always talking about how they are "off men" and are "happy being single." Dad isn't really into them, but he is polite. When my mother's folk festival friends are all busy being drawn to his energy, Mom gives him this "You old charmer" look and seems quite pleased that she has such a foxy husband.

On another note, I continue to make progress reading *The Fellowship of the Ring*. I'm on page five. I really understand now why it's such an important book. I can't believe I didn't read it sooner!

August 4
What a relief to have a session with Death Lord Bob after that scarring experience at the Grocery Giant. Let's see, we spent about five, maybe even ten minutes on the topic of my hair and my new look, then the rest of the hour either talking about Bob's friend Charles or just staring at each other.

When I walked in, Bob seemed taken aback. Then, obviously gathering up all his counselor training and internal resources, he took a deep breath and started. He leaned forward in his chair and stroked his goatee thoughtfully for a second.

"Well," he said.

Not knowing how I was supposed to respond to that overly open-ended counseling gambit, I said nothing.

Furrowing his eyebrows, which are, incidentally, suspiciously lighter than his jet-black hair, he tried again.

"Wow," he whispered, "that's quite a change."

"Yeah, I guess," I said.

Bob's goatee stroking was practically violent at this point. His mouth twisted as he racked his brain to remember the part in the counselor training manual that discussed how to deal with bad haircuts and fashion crimes.

"So that's sort of a different look for you, isn't it?" he whispered in his most intimate tough-guy voice.

I don't know whether I was supposed to feel special that he noticed or what. So I just shrugged.

Apparently Bob wasn't clear on whether he should bring into the open the fact that I looked terrible, or whether it would come as some sort of a devastating surprise for me. Bob shifted around in his seat. He crossed and recrossed his legs and smoothed his pant legs around his Doc Martens.

"So, how have you been? You know, since your new . . ." He trailed off briefly and then tried again. "Yeah, so how do you . . . ?" Another dead end. "Well, I think it's really great that you are developing your own, um, style." He let out his pent-up breath in a blast. "When does school start?" he finally asked.

I shrugged again and looked at him.

I guess Death Lord didn't know whether he should be trying to build up my poor self-esteem or whether it was his responsibility to get honest with me about how I really looked, you know, for my own good. And frankly, I was in no mood to help him out.

Before I knew it, Bob was halfway through the story of some friend of his who, a few years ago, had gotten seriously into blaxploitation movies from the seventies. This friend, Charles, had been inspired to get an afro in his shoulder-length light-brown hair. Bob said that it's really great to express yourself, an art really, if you think about it, but Charles's afro wasn't appreciated by everyone. In fact, Charles was teased so much about his afro (which apparently stood a full two feet off his head) that his self-esteem and his ability to interact with others on an equal basis were seriously damaged. And Charles didn't get platform boots with goldfish in the heels or anything—it was just basically the 'fro and a rugby shirt—but still the fashion experiment was not a positive experience for him. Plus, Charles was already established with friends and everything when he did his experimenting or it could have been worse.

By the end of the story, Bob was leaning so far forward and his whisper was so strained that I was actually worried about him. He had a death grip on his goatee.

"So you see, it's great to explore your personal style, but not everyone is going to appreciate, you know, the creativity behind it. Especially people that don't know you. You see?"

"Yeah, I guess," I said.

"So you see what I'm saying then?" He looked at me hopefully, if a little desperately.

"Yeah. People didn't like Charles's hair."

"That's right." Death Lord stopped for a moment and kind of slumped in on himself. We sat in silence, listening to each other breathe.

By the end of the session we had covered all the sick dynamics in Charles's family of origin and how Charles was actually the reason, mostly, that Bob had become a counselor, and how all this was really bringing up a lot of issues for him (Bob). When I left, he was being comforted in the waiting/recreation room by one of the hovering social workers and a couple of troubled teens.

I am sort of enjoying Bob's very indirect counseling style. He's trying hard not to pull a Mrs. F. and scar me for life by telling me what he really thinks. I appreciate the effort. I really do. But I can't help him out. I mean, what if I opened up and it caused him to pull a crackup like Mrs. F? I couldn't live with myself. And truth be told, I don't think I would really know what to say to Bob anyway. That I used to think I was a hobbit but it turns out that I might be nothing interesting at all? Besides, he's so nervous about me going back to school that I don't think he can take any more stress.

Later

Should have known. Bob put in a call to the guidance counselor at the high school as soon as I left. Then he called to tell my parents that he checked and Linda is not a student at the Alternative. She's been kicked out of school forever for beating up a small teacher. So that problem's solved. And he's warned the guidance counselor that I'm in an experimental phase and to be on the watch for any problems related to my hair. At least I think that's what he said. My mother is still not speaking to me, so my dad passed along the message, and he's not completely reliable.

On a more personal note, it's been only three days and already my pants are starting to give me a rash. That must be why people started wearing natural fabrics again. Also, the orange sleeveless muscle shirt isn't warm enough in the evenings, so I've been wearing it over a plaid shirt. As a look, it's not really happening. I have to do something about my fashion statement before school starts. I wish Frank would come back so I could get some more pointers from her. She looked stylish but I just look weird. Can I cross off number 7 on my Life Goals list? I mean, I have established an individual look. It just isn't very attractive. No, that's probably cheating. I'll just modify it.

Life Goal No. 7: Develop new look. (Like career choice, must reflect uniqueness. Must also be at least semipresentable, not just sad.)

PRINCE GEORGE, POPULATION:
70,000 OR SO; MALLS: SEVERAL;
NUMBER OF VIOLENT TEEN OFFENDERS:
UNKNOWN

August 6

My mother is speaking to me again. She sat me down today for the big talk about how hurt she was by the scene at the Grocery Giant. She says she's very worried about me, since school hasn't even started yet and already I'm running into some of the same problems as I did in first grade. Plus she wasn't sure I was "hitting the mark" with my new look. I considered mentioning that I wasn't exactly bursting with pride at her performance at the Grocery Giant or her overall fashion sense, either. After all, she'd just inflicted on me the single most traumatic experience of my life. Just so long as she doesn't try to pull me out of therapy with Death Lord due to lack of results. That would be a shame, especially now that he's really starting to open up.

Near the end of our talk, Mom got into the whole "How are you feeling?" thing. I think she assumes anyone as strange as me must be on the verge of suicide most of the time. God, these talks are such a drain. She gears up for them for days and never fails to end up in tears the minute she opens her mouth, which is something I could totally live without. I think she thinks that the way I am is something I'm doing to her. I can't believe how icky (that really is the only word for it) these conversations make me feel. She never lets up until she thinks we've gotten things solved or at least made some progress. She said how much she wanted to be supportive when school starts, but I'm going to have to "let her in."

Between her concern and Bob's anxiety, I'm starting to get a little worried about going back to school myself. But I can't be an invisible, stay-at-home, plaid-shirt girl forever. I have a life to live, and it's high time I met some people my own age who don't wear antlers.

After my mom finished crying, and telling me how much she loved me but didn't understand me, she suggested a trip to Prince George. We're going to stay overnight in a hotel, get new clothes for school, and get my hair fixed by a hairdresser who can do more than one style. I've heard about families who do these trips to the city before school. I never imagined my anticommercial mother would go for it. She must feel really bad. It's incredible that she's ready for another mother-daughter shopping trip already. People are still being interviewed by the police about the last one.

Can you imagine the trouble we could get into in Prince George, which is a real city with malls and freeways and probably hundreds of people who are as bad as Linda or worse? It boggles even a critical mind like mine.

August 10
Big news at the MacLeod house: My brother MacGregor had babies this morning. At least his angelfish did.

Mom spotted the eggs first, a sprinkling of tiny almost invisible balls, on the biggest leaf of the sword plant. She squealed and flew off to get MacGregor. Even Dad became animated. He kept saying, "Well now, this is quite the occurrence. A momentous occasion, really," between sips of his coffee.

MacGregor and Mom rushed back in a panic. It really was an emergency, because the angelfish pair have this nasty habit of eating their own eggs. When they first began spawning, MacGregor tried to allow the eggs to hatch naturally so the parents could raise the babies because, according to him, "cichlids are some of the best parents in the fish world. And watching them raise their fry is remarkable." Well, his angels are seriously faulty. They do their fascinating behavior–fanning the eggs and so on–for about an hour or two and then they have a big meal. It's disgusting, really. MacGregor says their natural brood-care behavior may have broken down because of inbreeding or because they feel threatened somehow. I say those fish are mutants. Their own eggs are a staple part of their diet, which is pretty sick when you think about it.

Since his fish are such crappy parents, MacGregor has decided to interfere in the natural order of things to protect the rights of the children. He is going to hatch the eggs himself. Time was short, because since the little cannibals have gotten used to the joys of infanticide, they barely even make a show of angelfish parental behavior. MacGregor says that usually one of the parents does a lot of shimmying up and down the leaf where the eggs cling, fanning them so they get enough oxygen, while the other angelfish stands guard, but with these horrors, it's out one end and in the other. After they eat their own potential offspring, the two of them have these extremely violent fights where they lock mouths and battle back and forth and upside down all around the tank. I wish it was more surprising that such a dysfunctional pair of fish ended up in our house.

While all this rough *Wild Kingdom*-with-Lorne Greene material unfolded, MacGregor sprang into action. He had a tiny little nursery tank already set up nearby, and he put some water from the birthing tank into it, plugged in the heater and aerator, and added some kind of blue chemical to the water. Then, with us standing around giving him suggestions like "Get them out quick!"–"I think they're going to attack!"–"I think you just blew it," and so on, he clipped the leaf with the eggs on it and transferred it into the small aquarium. MacGregor put the clipped leaf and eggs quite close to the bubbles coming from the aerator. The operation went smoothly, probably as a result of my good advice.

After the eggs had been medevac'ed out, I enjoyed watching the evil angels peering around, the cycle of child abuse broken. They tried to have their usual posthatch fight, but without the main cannibalizing event first, their hearts didn't seem in it. They made a few runs at each other, frayed a fin or two, and then returned to cruising back and forth between the swordplants.

I guess MacGregor saved the day, although letting such a pair of defects have children strikes me as a bad idea. I wonder what my brother could accomplish if he put his attention toward a worthwhile species. You know, like mammals. I think he could win a Nobel prize someday. Fish are a waste of his talents.

Anyway, the wait is on to see if the eggs hatch. Good thing my social calendar isn't too booked up. Between waiting for water to boil and my brother's eggs to hatch, I'm pretty much on a tight schedule. Plus I have about ten thousand pages of *The Lord of the Rings* to get through. *The Hobbit* may be a kids' book, but I sure made better time on it. I seem to be stuck on page fifteen of *Fellowship*. Maybe I should skip to *The Two Towers* and see if I can make a dent in that.

August 14
The whole family's been trying to get into the miracle-of-birth thing with MacGregor's angelfish. It's hard to get too excited about it, though, since the eggs and even the leaf they sit on are barely visible because the water has so much of that antifungal blue stuff in it.

Sometimes MacGregor is just great. He thinks I should get a fish tank because I'm interested in his. Actually, I'm mostly just interested in MacGregor. It must be really nice to be into nature instead of society and culture and the problems of the world, like I am. And there are probably a few more jobs in the nature field than in the the-world-sucks-and-I-don't-want-to-participate field. I think that my path as a student of life, cultural critic, and achiever of multiple Life Goals is much harder.

Tomorrow we head to Prince George. I wonder if the other families who make the big trip to Prince George for back-to-school clothes have to endure sage-burning ceremonies for safety beforehand and a father making cracks about how you haven't felt bad vibes until a bald tire blows. I think it's safe to say that we are the least sophisticated family in Smithers and possibly the entire Bulkley Valley Lakes District.

August 15
So far the trip to Prince George is just long. We left at about seven A.M. It's seven thirty now. My mom and I don't have much to say to each other. She wanted to know what kind of clothes we are looking for. I told her that I want stuff like what I have on. (I wore my stretch pants, muscle shirt, and down vest.) I don't think that's exactly what she had in mind. I bet she was hoping I'd want to get a few free-flowing hippie muumuus in pink and purple. Not likely. Thank God MacGregor is with us. He's supposedly getting fish equipment and some new clothes for school, but they

always bring us both on all major outings because they think he's a stabilizing influence on me. Now if we could just find someone to be a calming influence on my mother. After all, she's the one who gets into fights.

All three of us are going to some hair stylist recommended by Dad's gay friend, Finn. Finn plays poker with my dad and a few other town misfits. I have concerns about Finn's style suggestions because the only fashionable thing about him is his homosexuality. His clothes certainly aren't the last word in good taste. He wears these really cheap shoes from Zellers, the kind with fraying vinyl tassels and peeling soles. He is supposed to be anticonsumerism or something. He'd be better off barefoot than in the shoes he wears.

Finn has the glamorous job of Used Sporting Goods Salesman. He drags sweaty old jockstraps around and tries to sell them to truly unfortunate people. It's quite telling that business is thriving in this town. People in Smithers are so cheap, they're practically lining up to buy Finn's stinky wares. He is supposed to be traumatized by living in such a bigoted place (according to Dad), but from what I've seen, being gay in Smithers just makes Finn popular—at least with all the hippies and people who think they are too cosmopolitan to fit in here. It's kind of strange that people who've lived here their whole lives still think they don't fit. Probably their parents didn't think they fit either.

I once mentioned that theory to Mrs. F., and she said that was a very judgmental and inappropriate thing to say coming from someone who had never even driven a car or "taken a chance on love." The more I think about Mrs. F., the more I appreciate Bob.

Anyway, I hope that this "fabulous stylist" won't do an Irma on me. My hair has grown out a bit, but it still takes three or four heavy plastic barrettes to hold down the lump on top.

God, will we ever get there? Any minute now Mom is sure to make me switch places with MacGregor, moving me into the front seat so we can really bare our souls to each other. I've packed all three volumes of *The Lord of the Rings* and will be forced to pick one up and read it if my mom won't leave me alone.

Later

The Tropicana Inn is fancier than any hotel we've got in Smithers. It's got an indoor pool and a lot of palm trees and ferns and fountains and stuff right inside it.

We're supposed to go for lunch in a few minutes at the restaurant downstairs. Mom's acting girlish and giggly. I guess it's a treat for her to stay anywhere other than a free campsite, which is where we usually end up when we go on vacations. I will try to be nice and get along. MacGregor is already poking around in the plants by the pool. He says that it's interesting that tropical plants can live this far north and something about all the windows making the hotel act like a greenhouse.

I think I'll have breaded zucchini sticks for lunch. It's my favorite in a restaurant. Mom keeps us on a steady diet of stir-fried tofu and vegetables at home, so I try to make a point of going deep-fried whenever we eat out, which is pretty much never.

Still Later

We went to a whole bunch of stores this afternoon. It was very tiring. We spent about forty seconds getting MacGregor his new school clothes: cords and a couple of checked shirts—he's not very particular. Then Mom kept trying to steer us into stores filled with mucky-colored shapeless cotton dresses and African statues with big stomachs and little heads. Finally she just started going in and buying stuff for herself, not even making an effort to look like we were shopping for me. MacGregor went in with her and gave his opinion, which pretty much consisted of "That looks nice, Mom." My brother is a lot of things, but he's no critic. I waited outside on the sidewalk. She wouldn't have wanted my opinion.

She got a pair of saggy-bum pants and two droopy shirts with blue and purple splotches and a dress with red and purple splotches. She also got a couple of scarves with old-dishrag-looking smears of white and yellow and a big-bellied statue. It's a good thing *she'll* be all set when I go back to school after a ten-year absence.

She said that tomorrow will be my day for sure. We are going to find some thrift stores and stores with nonhippie clothes and go to the aquarium superstore, which, according to MacGregor, has over five hundred tanks of fish to choose from. I think we should also go to a mall, but Mom's against malls. I am too, in theory, but as a cultural critic I really should know my way around one.

August 16

It's no wonder the palm trees are thriving in this stupid hotel. It really is a greenhouse. I didn't sleep at all last night. It's so humid from the pool that everything feels wet and smells like chlorine. The crappy old air conditioner is on full blast, so not only is the room wet, it's also completely clammy. And the rattling is deafening. I woke Mom up a couple of times to ask her how she could sleep, but she was unsupportive and unhelpful. MacGregor suggested that I try sleeping in the tub, because the bathroom might be quieter, so I did, but when Mom got up to go to the bathroom, she screamed and woke me up.

I'm going to go swimming as soon as the pool opens.

God, I'm tired. The Tropicana Inn sucks. This trip sucks.

I am never going to accomplish any Life Goals on a trip with my mother and brother. The best I'll get is marginally better traveled.

Later

Well, that was certainly disgusting. So much for my pre-breakfast swim. There was a noticeable yellow tinge in the pool. I mean, it was that standard blue pool color and everything, but I bet every kid under fifteen who'd been in there had peed. Why else would they have to put so much chlorine in the water? My eyes look like the eyes of a habitual drug user. Maybe that will help me get a haircut like Frank's.

I swear some of those kids got in that pool just to go to

the bathroom. They got up, stretched, and went down to the pool to pee. I know MacGregor didn't, but then my brother is far superior to the average kid. He didn't see the yellow tint in the water either, but he has a tendency to see only the good in a situation. Mom didn't go swimming. She prefers a "natural body of water," which is just basically fish pee without the chlorine, as far as I'm concerned. It's almost enough to put me off my breakfast. But I've been looking forward to non-whole wheat pancakes since last night, and we'll probably need our strength for our hair appointments.

I pray this stylist friend of Finn's isn't another butcher. Well, even if he is, I haven't got all that much hair left to massacre. Our appointments start at eleven o'clock, and afterward we're supposed to go thrifting and then to Mac's fish store. I bet most people don't thrift with their mom and younger brother, but oh well. Just so long as Mom doesn't go and buy up every relic from the sixties. I wonder if thrifting counts as a life experience.

Later

I'm a new woman. This has been the best day of my life. I love Prince George.

It can only get worse.

I don't know where to start.

We went to Finn's hairdresser friend after breakfast. His shop is called MacGee's Frolic. I can't believe he gets any customers at all with a name like that. It sounds like a dog-grooming shop. Anyway, his name is MacGee, and from what I saw, he really likes to frolic. We arrived right on time but MacGee wasn't in yet. There was a receptionist at the front desk, asleep with her head on her arms. She had exactly the hair I wanted, and she was wearing a racing-stripe sweater, platform sneakers, and tight, checked stretch pants. You can imagine my relief!

We sat around for a while, and every so often Gilda, "I'll be assisting MacGee today," would lift her head and assure us that MacGee would be in soon. MacGee must like to spend time at work after hours. There were wine glasses everywhere, with cigarette butts floating in them and butts all over the floors and the counter and an empty gin bottle lying in the wash-up sink.

Mom said the shop smelled like a bar that the busser forgot to clean up. She didn't look very impressed.

Finally, at about a quarter to twelve, MacGee showed up. He certainly has different taste than old Crappy Shoes Finn. I think he may have been wearing the outfit he went to bed in. His shoes were pointy and made of shiny black leather, and his pants were pinstriped and Rod Stewart tight. The craziest part of his outfit was this see-through black shirt covered with fat, pink, fleshy-looking roses. The shirt had ruffles down the front and was buttoned up wrong, so there was a big gap open at his middle. His belly button was pierced. Oh my God! It was great!

MacGee's hair was bleached yellow and stood up in every direction. He still seemed pretty drunk, and his nose was that red only really serious drinkers get. Still, he was very good-looking.

He came striding in like he'd been running around all day and was totally exhausted. In a strong Irish, or maybe it was Scottish, accent he started in at Gilda for not "keeping my bloody appointments straight. Jesus, this is a business, lass. No room for unprofessionalism." When Gilda started to pout, he backed off.

"Oh Christ. All right. Just wake up. Keep it together. Lord Jesus, but my head hurts. Get me a coffee, would you?"

Then he turned to us with a huge smile.

"Well now. And how are we today? Aye, welcome to my frolic, my name's MacGee. Jesus, but you lot need some help, eh?" he said, looking from me to my mother.

My mother started to tell him that I was the one to be styled and how I'd recently had a bad experience, but she was just fine, thanks. MacGee was having none of it.

"Oh me darlin', I know just the thing for you. And the little miss here. Lovely. A bit of strangeness for a crown now, but we'll soon fix that. Oh yes, lass, you'll be a sensation. Look like a London girl, you will. And the young gent. A bit of the J. Crew naturalist look for you."

And back to my mother: "Quite a butcher you've had at the offspring, eh? And I suppose you'll be wanting a bit of an update?"

He turned away and clapped his hands.

"Gilda, me darling. We'll be needing help. It's a rush we've got here. Call young Lancelot. He'll be just the thing to get me through this morning." And to us: "Such a pity young Lance is underage. Lovely boy."

Soon Mom, MacGregor, and I were all sitting with our backs to the washing sink while Lance (a fresh-faced farmboy in a plaid shirt and Wrangler jeans) and Gilda ran around getting the right shampoos and conditioners.

MacGee sat in the corner on a high stool, chain-smoking and taking huge gulps of his coffee. He yelled out directions and complaints at the same time.

"My God in Heaven, Gilda! Chamomile for the lady and pine for the lad. Oh Jesus, my head. This is no ordinary hangover, I tell you. Likely I've developed a brain aneurysm, or some such.

"Our Father in sweet Heaven above, Lance, love. That's lemongrass. Pine, I said. Pine. It's the only thing for a young man who wears gum boots on a Saturday in town."

After about ten rounds of washing, rinsing, conditioning, rinsing, and clarifying, we were allowed to sit in the chairs on the other side of the shop. I was worried that MacGee had exhausted himself screaming out the washing instructions, but he was just getting going.

Soon we were all settled in our chairs, covered with shoulder towels and draped in huge plastic capes with a chili-pepper motif, and MacGee had a coffee in front of each of us.

"Lord God above us, Gilda! Get the lad a coffee. If he's old enough to grow hair, he's old enough to drink coffee. A bit of cream and sugar?"

And with a devilish wink at my mother: "Never too early to get 'em started on the vices, eh? Ha ha!"

Then MacGee got up and began sort of stalking around our chairs, glaring at our stringy wet hair. He would go all the way around, do a little pirouette-type thing, and go back around again. Hands on hips, he occasionally moved in and flicked at a piece of hair like it had personally offended him.

Finally he went back to his stool in the corner and furiously smoked another cigarette. Lance and Gilda stood at attention behind us. Even though Gilda was fully awake, she swayed back and forth a bit and did a lot of eye blinking. It was very exciting. Even MacGregor seemed interested.

Just when the tension was almost too much, MacGee lurched around, grabbed some scissors, and moved in on MacGregor's head. He was a hairdressing sensation with a tumorous shirt and red nose. Hair flew everywhere, and when MacGregor hunched down in his chair, MacGee stood back and pointed, and Lance pulled MacGregor up by the shoulders.

Before we knew it, it was over. MacGee switched to Mom.

She was a bit braver than MacGregor and didn't have to be pulled up by her shoulders. It was incredible to see the Relic of the Sixties meet the Scissors of Advance.

MacGee had a crazed but rapt look on his face. It must be a hairdresser's wet dream to get at a style-free zone like my mom's head. If anything, MacGee was cutting Mom's hair even faster than he had MacGregor's, bobbing in and out and dancing around. He started to sweat, pure alcohol it smelled like, and I was hoping that he wouldn't collapse before he got to me.

Finally, he went into this double pirouette with a dip from Gilda (I think she actually mopped his forehead) and lunged at me. It was the most terrifying experience. The scissors were inches from my eyes, little puffs of spray water hit me like tear gas, and sopping bits of hair fell everywhere. I could barely open my eyes for fear of losing my eyelashes. Every so often Gilda thrust one of those big fuzzy brushes at my nose or cheek, only to be repelled by the crazed, sour-smelling MacGee. He was no Irma. He was the real thing, faster even than Vidal Sassoon.

When he was finished, he slumped into his corner and I saw him pour something from a little flask into his coffee. He lit another cigarette and, with a trembling hand, pointed weakly at the blow-dryers. Gilda and Lance pulled massive hair dryers from their holsters and went at Mom and MacGregor with an abandon that suggested they had no clue at all what their hairstyles were supposed to look like.

Suddenly chipper after his coffee, MacGee came over and grabbed a hair dryer. He waved it all over the place while he gestured and talked about the lack of appreciation he got as an artist in Prince George. Blasts of hot air were directed at my ear or my eye for a second or two, and then at the floor or ceiling as he railed against the "bloody provincials, but God how I love the mountains and the open sky."

That kind of surprised me, since MacGee looked as

though he stepped outside only to get to the bar next door. He was one of the most unhealthy, un-outdoorsy-looking people I've ever seen. For an older guy, though, he was very attractive. Health is actually fairly overrated in appearance, I find.

Anyway, in spite of his total inattention to how my hair dried, it started to take on a shape. It was exactly what I wanted. It was just like Frank's and Gilda's. It was perfect! There is a limit to how excited I can get about something as shallow as a haircut, but I have to admit it was exciting to have my alternative hair vision brought to life by an artist like MacGee.

Mom and MacGregor, in spite of Gilda and Lance's total incompetence (I wonder if everyone back on the farm knew Lance was working in a hairdressing shop), also looked great.

Mom's was actually almost nice—a real revelation after her standard unrecovered hippie-do. MacGregor looked amazing—preppy, studious, and outdoorsy, maybe related to James Spader in some capacity.

I hadn't been that happy since I became conscious for the first time, you know, when I became aware of myself and got so uncomfortable and everything. I can't fail at school with hair like this! I'm becoming the person I want to be. In fact I was a little worried about all that joy, so I kept my face still. It's not a good idea to let on about extreme happy feelings. People get ideas. When Gilda came over and put a couple of metallic pink barrettes in my hair, my face slipped into a bit of a smile, but I caught it pretty fast. I think Mom saw, though, because even when she saw the bill, and our haircuts cost almost as much as our car, she didn't complain.

When we left, MacGee waved blearily from his corner, where he was alternating between his flask and his coffee cup. I think he said something about us looking fabulous, but he was talking into an empty space in the middle of the shop. Maybe he was congratulating himself on being fabulous or remarking again on the mountains.

Later

Oh my God.

I think I met a boy. Just saying it makes my skin crawl. I mean, it's so un-alternative or something. My boot face hasn't exactly attracted boys, guys, or whatever, to me like flies. Plus, there's that whole not-leaving-the-house thing. The whole girl-boy subject is embarrassing and dumb. Maybe I should be against it. And I am really, for the most part. God. I know I put that boy/girl interaction thing on my list. I know it's supposed to be normal. I just don't think I'm there yet.

We were in this store called Thrunge—I guess to capitalize on the whole grunge thing (so over now, but maybe the store can't afford to get its signs changed every time the music scene changes) and the whole thrift thing.

Mom and MacGregor and I were thrifting. I was finding some really great stuff. Velour V-neck shirts, a striped ski sweater, checked polyester pants, a silver vest, old housedresses, horn-rimmed glasses, lunch buckets with Bam Bam and Pebbles on them. I even found a pair of blue cord gauchos. I think my new haircut drew the cool clothes to me. I knew that once I looked alternative, I would attract alternative things into my life. And it was true.

I was just encouraging MacGregor to try on a *Charlie's Angels* T-shirt, and my mom was talking earnestly with the body-piercing specialist about "how we approached primitivism in the sixties," when this guy, boy, whatever, said "Hi" to me. Oh my God.

He was, it sounds juvenile and idiotic to say, I mean, enthusiasm isn't really my thing, but he was really cute. He told me he liked my hair. He told MacGregor that the *Charlie's Angels* T-shirt was cool, but maybe the G.I. Joe shirt might be better. He asked me where we were from. He asked me if I wanted to "go for a soda" and winked and said, "in the truest Kim Mitchell sense," and I had no idea what he meant, but I went anyway.

Oh my God. I was dying. Mom got really gushy and supportive but tried to act cool when I told her I was going to go out for a coffee or whatever while they went to MacGregor's fish store. It was painful. His name was Aubrey. He was wearing stretch pants and horn-rimmed glasses and a cardigan. I couldn't even talk. It was amazing.

We went to this diner-type place with these blond waitresses who were way older than my mom, even. They called us honey. It all felt very American truck stop.

Anyhow, I think Aubrey might be a sociopath. I mean, he is very confident for a seventeen-year-old. He wants to be a "low-fi musician," which I think means that you don't have to know how to play your instrument that well or be a very good singer. He said he "revels in misanthropy, but in a wholesome way." I couldn't help thinking about Ted Bundy. I guess that not all sociopaths are serial killers. I read somewhere that sociopathism can be very good in certain kinds of careers. And Aubrey isn't necessarily a sociopath–I just sort of wonder why he would want to have coffee with me. He said that he doesn't often get to meet people who think like he does and he could tell I do. He feels the same way about head bangers that I do about hippies. He said that hardly anyone buys Thrunge's cool clothes except him and the other guys in his band. I think Aubrey may have cultural critic tendencies too.

It was kind of shocking to meet someone as maladjusted as me. Mom always says my tendency to focus on the worst case negatively impacts my experience of life. Translated into English, that means she thinks I should be more positive. She may be right. It probably isn't normal to think that having coffee with a boy is automatically going to turn into a murderous spree. I guess deep down I think that most boys might be killers. Especially ones who dress like some kind of head-on collision between the fifties and the seventies.

Anyway, Aubrey assumed we had the same "worldview" based on my nodding head. I have never felt so sick in my life. I don't care about this stuff. I'm not even sure I'm a girl. I'm an eye in the sky. I am detached. I'm an idiot.

For a while I thought I was going to throw up. Was this

a date? Was I dating? Have I headed out into the sexual marketplace? I have nothing to sell.

I pulled it together when Aubrey asked for my phone number. He said he might cruise down to Smithers in his Pacer. By now he was calling me his soul mate in a totally over-the-top way. I was wondering if we were going to head off on a rampage, but he just grabbed my hand and walked me back to Thrunge. I may never recover. It was like an out-of-body experience. I'm an alien trying on human rituals.

I think I love Aubrey. I know I love my hair. I may even be a girl. The rituals of humans are very odd.

We got home at about nine o'clock at night. I am still changed. I didn't talk to my mom much on the drive back, but this time it wasn't because she was irritating me—I just had things on my mind. I think I'm radiating a combination of coolness and confidence. People are sure to notice the difference in me. And not just in my hair. I was feeling so alternative and mature on the drive home, I finished almost ten pages of *Fellowship*.

MINIMUM WAGE AT MOUNTAIN LIGHTHOUSE

August 17

I'm so depressed I can barely move. I don't think we natural depressives should get happy. It isn't good for us in the long run. My hair still looks great, though.

At the risk of sounding like an eighties hair band, I think this might be love.

Later

It's a good thing we weren't in Prince George any longer. Half the angelfish babies died while we were away. I guess they changed from eggs to little fish while we were gone and Dad didn't know how to handle it. They are still so small that you can hardly see them without a magnifying glass. They aren't swimming around or anything yet. They are still stuck by their tails to the leaf. Dad didn't know what to do, so he fed them brine shrimp (which MacGregor hatches in plastic jugs all over the basement). They were too young to eat the brine shrimp and the water got polluted and a whole bunch of the babies died. MacGregor got the nursery tank cleaned up, and now the rest of the baby fish look okay. He told Dad not to feel bad, that a certain amount of any hatch usually dies. Dad still feels bad. Luckily MacGregor doesn't go away that often. It's stressful on everyone not to have him running things.

Mom got a call from work tonight. She is the assistant manager at the local New Age/secondhand bookstore. Apparently one of the work study students walked out in the middle of her shift this afternoon, saying that she couldn't take another inane conversation about a bad writer with the local literati. I guess she was a student at the community college, or maybe even the University of Northern British Columbia, so she was quite intellectual.

Anyway, the store needs someone to take her place and Mom asked me if I would like the job.

The store is called Mountain Lighthouse Brambleberry Books. The owner is seriously into the principle of prosperity and loses no opportunity to save money, so she always hires the maximum number of summer students because the government pays most of their salaries. The fact that the store doesn't really need any help, which makes the summer students a pointless waste of money, even with the government subsidy, seems to have slipped under her prosperity scanner. Mom says that the idea is to help young people and give back to the community. I'm sure.

So it looks like I have a job. You have to wonder if they heard about my great haircut and stylish new clothes and thought I'd be good for business. I am knocking off items on that Life Goals list at an unbelievable rate. Maturity Indicators R Us over here. Just call me Alice Well-Adjusted MacLeod! I'm probably going to be the most mature person there when I go back to school. Yeah! Mom said I can take time off work to go for my counseling sessions. At this rate, who needs counseling?

P.S.

I wasn't going to mention this, since this is a journal of career exploration by a dynamic young person with limitless potential and an accounting of valuable Life Experiences, not the lovesick diary of some teenager, but Aubrey called today. We talked for over an hour. That is the longest I have ever stayed on the phone (not liking people and all). I think my parents were starting to worry that I'd had a stroke and was suffering some kind of paralysis.

Parts of the conversation were actually quite interesting. During other parts I read a bit of MacGregor's *Book of Amazing Animal Facts*. Aubrey is into conspiracy theories, and he said he won't be able to call for a while because "they" are going to cut off his phone service. I bet his marathon long-distance calls don't help. Probably the phone company doesn't accept paranoia about multinationals as an excuse for not paying your bills. I guess his parents got him his own phone line after their phone service was cut off a few times because Aubrey racked up huge bills calling Texas to hear some crazy guy's theories on phone company corruption.

Anyway, Aubrey's theory about AIDS (the CIA let it loose in humans after finding it in monkeys while researching biological warfare) is fairly interesting. Almost as interesting as the fact that the average mosquito has forty-seven teeth, or that the male duckbill platypus is the only venomous mammal in the world. In my only contribution to the conversation I told Aubrey I was reading all three books in *The Lord of the Rings*. He said he has them all more or less memorized and that he's heard that some people only ever read *The Hobbit*, if I could believe that. He laughed scornfully. So did I.

I haven't yet told my parents that he is coming to visit next weekend. I can barely deal with the idea myself. I'm sure we will have to have several embarrassing conversations about boys and girls, which, great hair and all, I'm in no mood for. Maybe Aubrey could stay somewhere else, and I could meet him there. Too bad I don't have a peer group.

August 18

Well, that wasn't so bad for a first day of work and everything. I mean, working in a bookstore isn't exactly a strain. The books don't need much attention, and if you pretend you can't hear the customer's questions, they just move on to the next student clerk.

Corinne, the owner of Mountain Lighthouse Brambleberry Books, trained me for about five minutes. Then she had to go and look after her chronic fatigue, fibromyalgia, and multiple chemical sensitivity disorder. Unfortunately for someone who owns a bookstore, Corinne is allergic to books and just about everything else in her store, including her customers and the native arts and crafts in the corner (the tanned rawhide makes her wheeze, and even the sight of feathers makes her swell up).

Fortunately, Corinne's husband is a doctor and they have quite a lot of money, so they built a huge special environmental house for her out of rare hardwoods and imported marble and special organic paints, which Corinne is able to tolerate very well.

My mom makes a big show of being very supportive of Corinne and all her illnesses, but I can tell it really burns her up that Corinne only works about an hour a week and she (my mom) has to do everything but is still only the assistant manager. I can see her point.

Today Corinne was wearing one of her see-through outfits. She has this collection of non-offgassing plastic jumpsuits tinted different colors, like purple and pink and green and such. Underneath she wears all-natural organic cotton pajamas. Mom says they aren't pajamas, but I know sleepwear when I see it. Apparently, the pjs cost $250 a pair and the jumpsuits are at least $500 each. Corinne has the jumpsuits made specially for her by the environmental materials unit at NASA. She wears the plastic suits only when she is feeling particularly "poorly," which is pretty much all the time.

Corinne also wears this Muslim veil-type thing with a floppy white hat. It's supposed to be some kind of all-natural face mask-air filter. She looks like an International Woman of Intrigue or one of the medical personnel from *Alien Autopsy.*

I guess the Mountain Lighthouse Brambleberry bookstore customers must be used to Corinne's problems, because they mostly stay away from her. If anyone gets too close, to ask a question or whatever, she starts to wheeze and holds out an arm and asks them to please step back. Then, with the back of one gloved hand against her veiled mouth, she gestures frantically like some futuristic Bedouin traffic cop for one of the other bookstore employees to come and help. Understandably, Corinne tries to avoid the part of the day when customers are in the store. She just basically shows up to count the cash float in the morning and then again at night to take the deposit.

Corinne showed me how to use the cash register and make change, and where the staff washroom was (right next door to the management washroom, which only Corinne can use because the organic cotton toilet paper and biodegradable, extra-pure, all-natural soap are so expensive). Then she rustled out the door to go home, which she refers to as "my cherished safe haven," and the most experienced work study student, Margaret, took over my training.

Margaret is very competent, you know; she really seems to know what she's doing. She is taking Native Studies at the college. Margaret is Native herself and very in touch with her heritage. To be totally honest, Margaret seems almost offensively together. She is relentlessly positive and political, but in a solution-oriented, win-win sort of way.

When my mom first started at the store, she was always coming home spouting the gospel according to Margaret. So I wasn't expecting to like Margaret. After all, my mother's taste is generally quite bad. And Mom doesn't just like Margaret; she treats her as if she's got a direct line to God. Margaret told her the distinctions between First Nations vs. Indian vs. Native vs. Aboriginal and what term can be used by who when. That kind of stuff is incredibly important to my mom. The funny thing is Mother can never quite remember the things Margaret tells her, so in an argument she always ends up getting all angry and frustrated and tongue-tied and saying, "It would make sense if you talked to Margaret—I can't explain it." And it's not just

Mom who worships Margaret. Everyone does. Dad says that Margaret is making a play for model minority status, but Mom says he's just cynical and possibly racist.

Much as I usually dislike nice, positive people, I have to admit that Margaret isn't bad. She has a decent sense of humor and everything. She showed me all the different sections in the store and cracked a few jokes about some of the flakier books. She even noticed my hair.

"That's a great haircut," she said. "I bet you didn't get that around here." And she said my Italian housedress was cool.

I hardly had to deal with any customers, partly because I avoided them and partly because they all wanted to talk to Margaret anyway. Most of the customers were long-hairs and quite of few of them carried big bags. I suspect that they were thieving from Mountain Lighthouse Brambleberry. They all looked pretty shifty to me, so I kept a close eye on them, except when they needed help. Then I pretended not to see them.

The best part of the day was when this young white guy with huge, long, clumped-up hair came in and was trying to impress Margaret with his First Nations know-how. He kept picking up stuff in the arts and crafts section and saying its name out loud in English and then in some Native Indian language that sounded like it was all vowels and qs. Then he chuckled to himself in a very self-conscious, knowing sort of way, obviously hoping that

Margaret was getting a good look at his action. Anyway, because of his huge hair, when the object fondler walked underneath the dream catcher display, speaking Quua- Qzluaa or whatever it's called, his hair got caught in the lowest dream catcher. The dream catchers are hung from the ceiling with fishing wire, so the one he was hooked on didn't fall off the ceiling when he got caught. Instead, it jerked him back by his hair and he gave this little (English) scream, and everyone, including Margaret, turned around to look at him, trapped by his hair. I almost felt sorry for him. Almost.

It was definitely my favorite part of the day. To get him untangled, Margaret had to cut off one of his two-foot-long braids. She assured him that people got their heads stuck to the dream catcher display all the time and that his braid was now a very special spiritual dream braid. And the object fondler left feeling very authentically Native and not all that much of an idiot. Margaret is the master, I have to say.

She laughed about it afterward, but not in a mean way. Her being so excellent makes me want to stop all the hip- pies from stealing. It's one thing to steal from Corinne, but ripping off Margaret is not okay with me. If she was to get disillusioned, it could be a blow to her morale and devas- tating to her community and everything. I want to do my part for race relations in this town.

So far the whole job thing is working out well. A boyfriend, school, a job—I'm not sure it's possible to get much more well-rounded. A few minutes operating a moving vehicle and I'm practically normal for my age. Take that, Mrs. Freison!

August 19

I got some visitors at work today. The boys who attacked me and my hair in the parking lot, Kevin and Jack, must have seen me here, because they came in to tell me that Linda would be out of treatment soon and she planned to kill me and my psycho mother.

Jack and Kevin are just lucky my mother was in Hazelton today buying more arts and crafts to litter the store. She would have kicked their asses. I didn't look up from my *Spy* magazine when they first walked in. That is my firm customer-service policy. If you start looking up, they start asking questions.

Kevin walked up to the counter and said, "Excuse me, Miss, but do you have any books about losers?"

I scowled at him. I also came up with some pretty clever replies, like "Yeah, in the section on your family history," but by that time he had been gone for about two hours so it lacked impact.

Jack snickered, and Kevin said, "I can't believe you have a job. You're too ugly to work."

I mumbled something about having to know how to read and they wouldn't know anything about that, but the words got tangled up and it just sounded like I didn't know how to talk.

Margaret must have been keeping an eye on them,

because she came over and asked if she could help them find anything. Kevin said, "Yeah. Sure. We are looking for some books on, like, violence and death." Margaret just looked at them steadily and said, "No. No, I don't think we have anything like that."

Then she turned to me and asked, "Everything all right?"

Margaret really is very cool.

Kevin and Jack looked sort of embarrassed and backed off, but before they left, Kevin told me that I was "dead meat" and that "no one is going to help you next time." Jack gave me a look I couldn't figure out.

After they left, Margaret asked me what was going on, and even though she is nice, or maybe because she is nice, I couldn't tell her. I said they were just some guys I knew and it was nothing. She said I could come to her if I ever needed to talk.

God, I hate this stuff. Maybe a career in the public eye isn't right for me. I just pray that, like Linda, Jack and Kevin have been kicked out of school forever too. There's no way I want to risk running into them at school.

Other than the touching visit by Kevin and Jack's Welcome Wagon contingent, work wasn't too bad. I almost caught a couple of people stealing, I think. One woman got all the way to the rebirthing section before I got her bag from her. She looked startled when I grabbed it, almost like she was going to put up a fight. Then for sure I would have known she was stealing. But Margaret came over and got her calmed down, and then asked me to go to the back and count the Stephen Kings, so I wasn't able to do any more theft prevention.

August 20
My career as a critic is poised to take off. All the pieces are in place. I have different clothes than everyone else, my hair looks great, and I am a disaffected-observer type. The problem now is what to criticize. I mean, it's not like there's any big lack of targets or anything. I could do music videos, monster tours by the oldsters of rock, the general horribleness of the taste of everyone in this town—you name it.

I'm a bit nervous about writing music criticism. I like alternative music, although I have to admit that I'm not a hundred percent clear on what it is. I think it means anything that isn't too successful. Aerosmith is not alternative. The Ass Ponys are. It's a little hard to keep up with it all while living in Smithers. The local Sound Man outlet only carries new country, Top 40, and the dregs of the sixties. Another obstacle to becoming a music critic is that I don't have any money for CDs. So basically I've just read about the music I like. I say I hate all the mainstream stuff, and I do, but mostly on principle. I assume that if a band is commercially successful, it must suck. Critics agree that the musical preferences of average people are terrible.

I completely agree, but I worry about my own taste sometimes. I'll hear a song and think it's really great, but then find out it's number one on the charts and have to change my mind. I should probably be able to tell mindless Top 40 from good music if I am going to be a critic.

I had a fairly demoralizing experience a while ago when I was baby-sitting for this yuppie couple. They were serious chart victims, and after putting their kid to bed, I started checking out their music collection and feeling pretty superior. I knew all the bands!

They even had a Britney Spears CD. I can't stand her music. I read that she is just a creation that some producer is foisting off on unsuspecting little kids who don't know any better than to be suspicious of someone who is such a good dancer. I mean, how likely is it that a person with her flexibility and abdomen would also be a good songwriter? She does not appeal to those who, like me, prefer more sophisticated, independent artists, like the Ass Ponys.

Somehow I convinced myself that if I was going to become a music critic, I should probably listen to her album. The kid was asleep, so he wasn't going to tell anyone that I had been listening to schlock. I now know it was a mistake. A real music critic wouldn't have done it. I guess I hoped that the record would be so sickeningly manufactured, so blatantly fake, that I would be unable to listen to the whole thing and then I would know that my taste wasn't as bad as most people's.

So I put it on. And damned if there weren't some catchy songs on there. I immediately got that I-feel-moved-I-think-I-want-to-dance feeling. I turned the stereo up and was sort of singing along and everything. I really got into Britney, but in a furtive, porno-reading kind of way. I even taped the whole album so I could listen to it on my headphones so no one could tell what I was listening to.

And it got worse. I put on an album by one of those boy bands. It was filled with stick-in-your-head type songs and really sort of romantic songs. I got all sing-alongy and was even doing a bit of dancing with a pillow.

I really hate myself sometimes.

Anyway, in the end I was sitting on the floor in the middle of a pile of all these mediocre CDs by popular bands. I was having a Top 40 orgy. And worst of all, I was trying to get them all taped so I could keep listening. It was sick, I admit. When Mr. and Mrs. Crappy Music Taste came home and found me like that, I felt pretty embarrassed, like I had been in their liquor cabinet. I guess for them it was mostly an issue of me stealing their blank tapes—which I can understand. They couldn't really be expected to know that their taste in music was the shameful thing. It didn't seem like the time to tell them.

It ended with them refusing to pay me and making me give back all their tapes. They didn't ask me to baby-sit again. Actually, no one has ever asked me to baby-sit again. I guess word has gotten around about my music problem.

THE PROBLEM WITH AUBREY

August 20

Aubrey is coming to visit in two days. That means I have to tell my parents. If I was honest, which I am clearly not, I would admit that it's not just the telling-my-parents thing that has me stressed; it's the whole boy-I-don't-even-know-visiting-me-and-staying-the-night thing.

I am not a people person. I could barely cope with coffee. Well, at least Aubrey isn't used to all kinds of witty conversation out of me.

Does he think we're going to act like young marrieds or something? Another five-minute session of hand-holding will do me in. And the thought of my family watching all our awkward how-do-you-do's is just too painful to consider.

I guess I'll tell my parents tonight. Maybe Linda will catch me on my way home from work and put me out of my misery. I can only pray.

Later

Work wasn't bad today, I guess. Both Margaret and my mom are always sending me to the back every time there is some little customer complaint. That's okay, since I find it tiring to monitor all the thieves.

Today I was crouching near the abuse/recovery

section trying to see through the shelves to the criminal-looking longhair on the other side who was spending way too much time with *Women Who Run with the Wolves.* For some reason Mountain Lighthouse Brambleberry has an unusual number of thieves. You can tell them because they behave very strangely, carry giant shoulder bags, and smell like patchouli. My dad suggested that the way the customers look and act "might be a function of being the kinds of people who shop at New Age/secondhand book-stores." Ha! It's a function of being up to no good. I read that shrinkage, which is a fancy name for stealing, costs small businesses millions. Not on my turf!

Take my suspect today, for instance. You have to wonder, when the men's movement section was com-pletely on the other side of the store, what this guy was doing in the women's psychological archetypes section. He was probably a pervert of some kind. Kneeling, watching him through the bookshelf, I was so focused that I didn't hear the customer coming up behind me. She didn't see me, either, because she fell over me, let-ting out a terrified howl as she went down, and my sus-pect fled, and all in all it was a bit of a scene. I bet the guy stole the book. I wouldn't be surprised at all. We should charge the woman who fell over me for it. My mom asked me (quietly) what the hell I was doing, and Margaret laughed and said there was some sorting left to be done in the back. I was just sorry the thief had escaped, and so nervous due to life circumstances that I could hardly keep the Dick Francis pile clear of the Sidney Sheldons after that.

Later

I finally told my parents about Aubrey's visit, and just as I expected, they were ridiculous. My mother tried to be loving and supportive, but her innately suspicious nature kept creeping in. It was like watching Sybil change personalities. "Oh honey, of course we'd love to have Aubrey stay." Then, "And where exactly will he stay? Hmmm?" Then, "Oh, I just think it's wonderful that you're meeting new friends." Then, "And his parents don't mind him staying here? I mean, they don't know us and he is very young." And on and on and on.

Dad was all raised eyebrows but didn't really say anything. So I guess that's it. Now he's going to come for sure.

People who date regularly must die young. This kind of stress can't be good for you. Plus this is going to slow down my Life Goals progress. Unless I add wife and mother to the list. Oh, never mind. I'm too torn up to even worry about going back to school. The stress is unreal. I'm practically bedridden. This visit feels like some kind of arranged marriage. We are like a couple of tribal youngsters sent out to the tent while the photographers from *National Geographic* watch.

Well, actually, judging by the height of Dad's eyebrows, we won't be spending any time in the tent or anywhere else alone, which is just fine with me. I am not a woman! I am not ready for any of the rites of womanhood! I can't afford to get involved!

August 22

Dad came upstairs this morning with a full itinerary for Aubrey's visit. He has every single minute of the weekend planned and typed up into a folded and stapled schedule. There is a booklet for each of us and one for Aubrey when he gets here. Dad asked me if I thought he should mail one to Aubrey's parents. I said I didn't think it would get there in time. I would be really annoyed at him if I wasn't so relieved. Not being a big one for having friends, I had no idea what I was going to do with Aubrey, you know, to entertain him.

Mom told Dad that the itinerary was a "masterpiece of compulsiveness." He said she was just too afraid to face that part of herself that wanted to do the same thing. I once heard Uncle Laird describe my dad's life as being "a remarkable combination of obsessive busywork and near-catatonic sloth." At the time my mom asked Uncle Laird where he got his medical degree, but today she seems to be agreeing with the diagnosis. MacGregor reviewed the schedule and said he didn't think fifteen minutes would be quite enough time for Item 2.3 (Option 1), Hike up to the Twin Falls, but that Item 2.3 (Option 2), Go See Gherkin's Pottery Studio, might be possible in that time frame, as long as we didn't get into any conversations with Mrs. Gherkin, who does like to talk.

I don't care really. I just don't want to be sent to the womanhood tent.

My stress level is affecting my judgment. Today, for no good reason, I felt annoyed at Corinne and so right before she was due to come in, I hot-boxed the storage room. I lit three sticks of Buddhist Temple Blend incense and closed all the doors and windows. I knew that she had to go back there to get the deposit book. Mom had gone home early and Margaret was busy with customers. No doubt about it, as far as career advancement goes, it was a bad move.

When Corinne went into the back room, she walked into a white cloud of Buddhist Temple Blend smoke. She staggered out, gasping and wheezing, with her huge white plastic-rimmed sunglasses all fogged up. She flung open the front door and ran out onto Main Street coughing and flailing her arms around. Margaret sniffed the incense and told me that I should probably call it a day. So I left out the back door while Margaret hooked up the Envirofan and pointed it at the storage room.

Probably wasn't the best idea. I have a lot on my mind.

Later

Aubrey is coming any time now. I am just sick.

Earlier today Bob said he was picking up some real feelings of anxiety from me. I guess his first clue was the fact that I was swilling from an economy-size bottle of Pepto-Bismol. He got all therapist on me and wanted to know if I was worried about returning to school. He re-assured me again that we'd get through it together. So I told him that made me feel better. Of course it was a total lie, but at least one of us felt more confident.

I wouldn't want Bob to feel like he wasn't "having an impact." He'll probably never wear anything other than all-black undertaker clothing if he doesn't have some suc-cess in his life. And since I'm going back to school as a favor to him, pretty much, you can't accuse me of not doing my part.

Later

Well, Aubrey's here. He's actually here. He got in at about seven o'clock, and my mother went into this terrible groovy sixties mama meets June Cleaver act. My dad smiled grimly and grabbed Aubrey's bags and took him down into the basement, where he would be staying.

Everyone was trying to pretend like I have friends–or boyfriends, I guess–come to stay with us all the time. They didn't know what to do with themselves. I admit I wasn't clear on how to handle the situation either.

Before my dad had a chance to implement the first item on his itinerary, which wasn't actually scheduled to begin officially until nine P.M., Aubrey asked me if I wanted to go for a walk.

The second we hit the driveway, Aubrey started to talk. And talk and talk. The drive was okay. It was really great to see me. His parents suck. His favorite Pavement album is *Slanted and Enchanted.* The other guy in his band won't rehearse. Is sex something that interests me at all? And on and on.

It wasn't so bad. I didn't have to say much because Aubrey wasn't looking for answers. I almost told him about going back to school after being taught at home for ten years, but I didn't get an opening. We walked down past the high school and around the civic center, then along the trail by the river. Then we walked home. We held hands.

I think Aubrey might have some kind of mental illness. I mean, he just says and does anything he wants. Whatever happened to being a paralyzed-by-fear teenager? And the weird thing is that Aubrey never really talks about the thing that he is supposedly talking about. Even when he's talking about something else, it's really always about him. It's not that attractive a personality trait. But still, it was nice to hold hands with a boy, guy, whatever, who wears fifties-looking checked shirts and drives a Pacer. It made me feel–oh, never mind. It was just kind of nice.

I realized partway through our walk that Aubrey probably wasn't going to try to take me to the womanhood tent. He could never stop talking long enough to do anything that physical. I guess that's a relief. Sort of. And I've basically accomplished Life Goal No. 4, the boy-girl-interaction goal. Consider that crossed off. This thing with Aubrey is more than enough boy-girl interaction for me at this stage.

My dad has him down in the basement again. I think they're discussing music or something. I have this feeling that Aubrey isn't going to notice when Dad goes into his Mr. Ironic mode. He should count himself lucky.

Later

Thank God that evening is over. It was actually one of the more unpleasant social occasions I have endured, which is really saying something considering some of the Bulkley Valley Lakes District Home School Collective events I've attended. We were supposed to have a Family Plus Guest card game, Item 1.2, but all we did was provide a captive audience for Aubrey. Me, my mom and dad, and MacGregor got all of Aubrey's thoughts on gambling, drugs, prostitution, and other vice squad-type offenses. I have to admit it was pretty boring, even though we're a new couple and I'm in the he-can-do-no-wrong, rose-colored-glasses stage of our relationship (at least I should be, according to the *Cosmo* article I read about how to tell if you are dating a psychopath or a stalker). Apparently this beginning part of our relationship is very dangerous and everything because I am so smitten that I am likely to overlook warning signs. Not likely. Unfortunately, I already have a good idea of just what is wrong with Aubrey.

Dad was getting quite nasty by about twelve thirty. He was saying things like "Yes, by all means share with us your thoughts on red-light districts, Aubrey. I'm sure they'll be as illuminating as your thoughts on corruption on the New Orleans police force from that piece you heard about but didn't get to see on *Sixty Minutes*. Please do go ahead."

Aubrey didn't notice and I felt embarrassed. I guess that's what they mean by codependence—when someone else's behavior makes you feel like an idiot, just because you know him. Leave it to me to go straight to the neurotic part of having a relationship. Judging from the descriptions of codependence I found in the book about detaching from the toxic person in your life that my mom keeps on her bedside table, pretty much everyone is codependent. If you are alive and conscious, you are probably codependent.

The cure, as far as I can tell, is to get "clear boundaries"—you know, the whole "that's your stuff, not my stuff" approach. If Aubrey's stupidity is making my skin crawl, I don't have to take it as some kind of reflection on my taste. I can just practice detachment. It seems to me that being non-codependent could allow a person to hang out with some real idiots and still feel good about herself. In the future if my mother tries to shame me with her disapproval, I will let her know in no uncertain terms that I reject her and all of her codependent baggage. I am Codependent No More.

Even though I'm in a place of healthy detachment and strong boundaries (or is it borders?), I'm still dreading tomorrow. Aubrey's almost enough to make me miss all those boys who don't know I'm alive.

August 23

This morning Dad implemented Saturday's schedule. He personally lasted only half a day before he went home to be in the basement. I guess he finally figured out that Aubrey will never be quiet long enough to get into any kind of teen sex situation. By midafternoon Mom had dropped her Hippie June Cleaver routine and was getting really foul-tempered. I got lots of practice in non-codependence.

After breakfast we went to the taxidermist on the Lake Road to look at the stuffed black bear and other works in progress. Mr. Crenshaw, the taxidermist, was in the middle of stuffing old Mrs. Kribenski's late chihuahua, Squeak. I find that domestic pets look even more fierce stuffed than wild animals. Old Squeak, with his little overbite and bug eyes, looked especially demonic. I guess the German shepherd from across the street must have got him, because Squeak was bald and cut up. Mrs. Kribenski obviously tried to have the vet save him—you could see the stitches and shave job looked professional. The plastic collar thing they put on dogs so they can't take out their stitches, that thing that makes dogs look like low-budget Martians, was still sitting beside Squeak on the taxidermy counter. Not much need for a hood now. He can probably be trusted not to hurt himself. I wonder if Mr. Crenshaw is going to take the gritty reality approach and have Squeak wear his hood while moldering into eternity. That would really help make him a conversation piece.

Anyway, Aubrey gave us all, even Mr. Crenshaw, a lecture on how taxidermy is bad because when animals are stuffed they lose their dignity or something. Apparently Aubrey read an article about Native spirituality and animal spirits and that kind of thing, and now he thinks he's one of the world's foremost experts on animal afterlife. About halfway through Aubrey's talk, Mr. Crenshaw gave a snort and said he didn't have "time for this shit." He stalked away muttering "the goddamn things are dead already, for Christ's sake."

Aubrey wasn't discouraged and after his lecture went and stared into the slightly crossed marble eyes of the moldy old black bear in the front hallway. I think I heard him whisper, "Courage, Brother Bruin," but I hope not.

Next on the agenda was a trip to the Igloo, Smithers' dome-shaped natural history museum. Unfortunately, the Igloo is one of the taxidermist's best customers and is full of stuffed animals. One display had a weasel poised to attack a beaver while an eagle, wings outstretched, looked on. Deep in Native spirituality mode, Aubrey gave the beaver a little scratch under the chin. He asked in a really loud voice, "How would we human vermin feel about the indignity of being stuffed and having our souls trapped on earth?" Dad pointed out that Egyptians used to pay top dollar for just that, then grumbled something about not being able to "take it anymore" and went out to sit in the car.

After we dropped Dad off at home, we went to the fossil beds. As we got out of the car, Aubrey went off on another tirade about honoring the spirits of the fossilized squished bugs and leaves.

My mom considers herself quite the environmentalist, so she tried to start a discussion about the earth as an educator, but Aubrey told her, "Sometimes sorry is just not enough." When Mom got mad, he made a big show of being even-tempered and told her that it wasn't his fault she felt guilty. Then *she* stomped off to sit in the car.

That left me and MacGregor and Aubrey to walk up to the double waterfall attraction. I was a bit worried that Aubrey would chain himself to a tree or something to protest what he was now calling "the zoo-merization of the wilderness." It was obvious that he was really into the new word, because he put it in just about every sentence.

"I think it's up to us young people to refuse to contribute to the zoo-merization of the wilderness."

"Look at all this zoo-merization."

and

"Zoo-merization is bad."

Even MacGregor was starting to look pained. Aubrey went so far as to say that he thought the rainbow from the waterfall's spray was zoo-merizing nature's beauty. I couldn't follow what he was talking about at all, but because I am Codependent No More, I just ignored him and, taking MacGregor, turned around to go and sit in the car with my mother. Unfortunately Aubrey followed. Given his social skills, I'm beginning to wonder if Aubrey was educated at home.

The nature events weren't going well, so Mom skipped Item 2.4 (Option 1): Short Hike to the Glacier and told us we were going straight on to Item 2.5: Eat Picnic

Lunch Outside Smithers History Museum. Lunch was standard my-mother fare—eggplant dip, sprout sandwiches, and some crappy-looking organic apples with brown spots from not using enough pesticides. We had to eat in the car because it started raining. Tensions ran high. Aubrey said he needed meat with a meal to feel like he'd actually eaten. Mom said that didn't sound "congruous" with the rest of his beliefs and that most people who care about the environment are vegetarian. Aubrey replied that hippies have been forcing their outdated morality on everyone for years and he, for one, was tired of it. Mom said that the holes in his worldview were so big you could "drive a truck through them," and he said "I'll never pander to the vegetarian fascists," and Mom told him that we (me and him) were a match made in heaven and made us get out of the car. Then she drove away. She made poor MacGregor get out too, which wasn't really fair, but I guess she wanted him along to make sure no teen sex happened.

So the three of us went into the museum to escape the rain. At least the regular history museum, unlike the Igloo, didn't have any stuffed animals. It's actually pretty good considering it's only one room. The stuff in it isn't really all that interesting or anything, mostly pieces of horse harnesses, a couple of farming tools, quilts, and some old photos, but if you cleaned all the old crap out, it would be the nicest house in town, with its wood floors and high ceilings and all.

I kind of like the museum because it feels old and secure. But Aubrey thought it was lame and upset the curator, Mrs. Morgan, by telling her that if she was a little less traditional in her approach, the museum could be more successful. She asked him what he meant, and he told her about some artist who did a sculpture of Jesus peeing and couldn't she try to get in some important exhibits like that. Mrs. Morgan told him that she was running a museum and not an art gallery, and he told her that her "tendency to make small-minded distinctions" was what kept the museum from being a cultural influence in a town that "badly needs it." Then she asked us to leave, even MacGregor, who she knows and likes because he has helped her with a few exhibits.

So we headed home. I held on to the lunch bags with both hands so I wouldn't have to hold Aubrey's hand. I was feeling pretty codependently sick of him. As I write this I'm hiding in my room.

I'm going to have to be boyfriendless. Aubrey is interfering with my burgeoning career as a critic. I can hardly criticize at all when he's around. He makes me feel like saying nice, positive things just to contradict him. That can't be healthy. Someone should tell Aubrey that critical people should speak only infrequently. That way it really means something.

Later

Aubrey drove off after dinner. I think he left because my dad told him it was "probably not a good idea to stay any longer." I was pretending to be sick and wouldn't come out of my room. MacGregor had disappeared into the swamp, and Mom had gone off to some folk-festival excuse-to-drink event. So I guess Dad thought he should say something to Aubrey after they ate dinner together.

When Aubrey knocked on my door, I told him that I thought I had the flu and asked him what the symptoms of the Ebola virus were. I figured that spewing black bile onto someone or gushing blood from every orifice, known to us virus fans as "bleeding out," would be enough to keep Aubrey away. He's pretty paranoid. I felt sort of bad, but I really needed to reestablish my borders.

So it looks like we aren't going out anymore. My hand-holding, girlfriend-being days are over. The whole boy-girl love thing is another area in which I am an island. I'm not sure how this development affects my list. I mean, do I have to reinstate Life Goal No. 4? I don't think so. Our boy-girl interaction probably ran its natural course. It doesn't have to be long-term to count. All I can hope is that someone from school saw Aubrey and me together so word gets out that I've got dating experience. No one needs to know about Aubrey's personality. He looks good, and in a situation like this, that's what's important.

THE DOWNWARD SPIRAL

August 24
Well. Everything is back to normal. No more Aubrey to be irritated by. I, for one, am devastated. My time as a

significant other was short-lived but intense. It was nice to be anxious about something other than being killed by Linda and going back to school, which is probably the third most hostile environment on earth after the deep ocean and Everest.

This may be a good time to take to my bed with depression. Dad does that frequently, and so do a lot of the women in the books I read. It sounds like a good way to handle problems. Sort of like lying down in the middle of the road and refusing to move. Freeing.

August 25

My mom came into my room last night while I was having my depression. She gave me a book about girls' bodies and how the world makes it hard for girls to accept themselves and how in the old days they weren't allowed to do much and had to wear a lot of underwear but at least they had drawing lessons and got to learn another language. Mom told me that she hoped the book would make me feel better. Actually, it just made me feel confused.

The book said that in modern society girls are "terrorized" by media images of female perfection and by unrealistic expectations about their bodies. It also said girls are led to believe that they are valuable only as sex objects for boys. I don't think I'm suffering from that particular delusion. I'm an object of ridicule, maybe, but that's about it.

Mom is always giving me these feminist books, and some of them are pretty good, but where I really learn about women is from her. The whole feminism thing is one area where I sort of respect my mom. She used to have this friend, not one of the folk-festival babes but a regular, working-in-the-office-at-the-mill type woman. This woman, Debbie was her name, used to come to our house after her logger husband would beat her up. Mom was actually pretty cool about it.

She would listen and ask Debbie what she wanted to do. You could tell that if she had started off telling Debbie to ditch her loser husband, Debbie would have just left, but Mom worked her around to the idea of changing things slowly. I can't really explain what it was she said to Debbie that I liked. I guess it was just that she was really gentle and respectful. If that's feminist, it's something I can get behind.

Debbie left her bad husband quite a while ago, and now she's married to a new guy. He's supposed to be okay. She never comes over anymore, though. I don't know why. Maybe she's embarrassed. It's too bad. I liked her more than most of Mom's other friends.

I should probably add "become practicing feminist" to the Life Goals list. I wonder if it involves anything other than being nice to other females. I can do that. Although it will be a challenge with some of my mom's friends.

I am almost ready for some new Life Goals since I'm knocking them out of the way like a championship bowler. Let's review:

LIFE GOALS LIST

~~1. Decide on a unique and innovative career path (to get helping professionals off my back).~~

~~1.a. Get part-time job in preparation for said career path? Too much like work? (Should be outside family home.)~~

2. Increase contact with people outside of immediate family. (Not friends, necessarily, but at least superficial interaction of the "Hi, how are you?" variety with people who are not home-based learners and do not attend the Teens in Transition Club.) (May have been accomplished with Aubrey. Although if anyone is a candidate for the club, it's him. Review in a week.)

3. Learn to drive a car (but not our car, because I do have my nonexistent reputation to consider).

~~4. Some sort of boy-girl interaction? (Possibly best left until after high school. Maybe best left until middle age.)~~

5. Publish paper comparing teenagers and chicken peer groups (in LANCET or other respected publication?).

6. Read ~~entire LORD OF THE RINGS series~~ Prologue to THE FELLOWSHIP OF THE RING to prove that early, parent-assisted reading of THE HOBBIT was not

just an aberration, and I really am advanced for my age. (Do not dress like the characters.)

7. ~~Develop new look. (Like career choice, must reflect uniqueness. Must also be at least semipresentable, not just sad.)~~

8. Go back to high school. (Leave the warmth and safety of home-based learning atmosphere. Do it to save the career and self-esteem of counselor.)

9. Become practicing feminist. (Find out what it entails besides being nice to other females. Subscribe to MS. magazine or other feminist magazine?)

August 26

Today was a seriously bad day, even by my standards. Getting fired by my own mother was actually the best thing that happened to me today.

I guess Corinne recovered enough from the Buddhist Temple Blend incident to use the phone, so she called up my mom at work and told her that I was not ever to come back, and that I should be gone by this afternoon. I knew something was up when I heard Mom stuttering into the phone.

"She did what? Oh my. Yes. Oh my. I am really sorry. Yes, yes. I can. . . . Yes. No, I understand. Complaints? Everyone? Oh dear. I am really so sorry."

I heard that and I just knew from the tone of her voice

and defeated posture and everything that the call was about me. So I went back to alphabetizing the Danielle Steeles that wouldn't fit on the shelf.

After the call, Mom headed out to the car to do some stress-relieving exercises. I always know when she is really upset because she goes out to the car and plays this tape with all these different kinds of jungle animal noises on it, like monkeys and cheetahs and elephants and parrots, while she squeezes sand-filled balls with her hands. It looks terrible. I wish she would do it someplace more private than the car. In fact, I wish she would take up jogging like the other mothers, but apparently this ball gripping is the only thing that makes her feel better. It's called jungle balling, and she said she was taught it by some breakaway sect of rolfers, and that it helps her to get in touch with her primitive self.

Anyway, after Mom came back into the store, all jungled out, she asked me to come over to the metaphysics section, which she is convinced is the most peaceful section in the store. Margaret must have known what was going on, because I could see her trying to keep customers corralled in the meditation section.

"I just had a talk with Corinne," Mom began.

So I said, "Oh yeah."

Mom was trying to keep one stern eye on me and one on the customers who kept breaking free of the meditation section and heading toward the metaphysics corner. She began performing breath of fire, the breathing technique she uses when she needs to focus. Why she didn't just fire me in the back room like a normal boss is beyond me.

"Alice, you should know that Corinne's health may have been seriously jeopardized by your stunt with the incense." Snort. Snort.

I shrugged.

"What were you thinking? What could possibly explain your actions? Carelessness? Because I'd hate to think it was intentional." Snort. Snort.

I shrugged again, still at a loss for anything to say, other than I was as mystified as anyone by my behavior.

By this time there were about four customers standing as close as possible to make sure they didn't miss a thing. One particularly idiotic woman stood watching us like we were some kind of community theater act, nodding every time my mom spoke. She only stopped when Mom snarled, "Get away" at her. Then she actually had the nerve to look offended. Margaret started calling out specials in the arts and crafts section in an effort to get people away from the scene of my disgrace.

A few more snorts and Mom got to the point.

"You realize I have to let you go now." Snort, snort. "I don't have a choice. I can't believe you've put me in this position." Snort, snort.

"So I'm fired?"

"Yes. You're fired. I, your mother, am going to have to let you go."

"Fired?"

"Alice, don't be obtuse. Not now."

Mom looked drained.

"I'm going to go get some lunch and run some errands. You might as well head home as soon as you finish helping Margaret." She gritted her teeth. "Corinne said she'd prefer you weren't here when she comes to close up."

So that was it. Fired by my own flesh and blood. No longer would I carry on the family tradition of being exploited in the local New Age/secondhand bookstore. I couldn't help thinking that Mom and Corinne would be sorry when all the thieving hippies got up to their old tricks without me there to stop them. Margaret came over and asked if I was okay. I told her I was fine and was just going to finish up some sorting in the back and get my things.

I'd thought lots of times about what my first firing would be like, and was a bit disappointed that I didn't have, like, any family photos and plants to put in a cardboard box to carry through the office while all the other desk jockeys looked on sadly and maybe a bit enviously. That is another reason retail sucks. It is hard to make a big exit. Once you are gone, you are as forgotten as any old customer.

I finished sorting fast because I felt sorry for Margaret, who looked quite concerned for me and everything. I decided to leave the mirrors I had brought in for surveilling, just in case Margaret decided to take over security. It was my grand and noble gesture. Maybe it wasn't all that grand, but it was fairly noble if you think about it. I said good-bye when I left, and she smiled and said something about a path winding around or something like that, and though it sounded pretty profound, I didn't get it and it would have spoiled the moment to get her to explain it.

When I stepped out of the store into the sunlight, I looked across the street and there, standing right outside the post office, were Kevin, Jack, and Linda. I said a little prayer that they hadn't seen me and made a split-second decision to take advantage of Death Lord Bob's invitation to come by anytime to hang uselessly around the club. I walked as quickly as I could, afraid to look behind me. *Don't run,* I counseled myself. I made it to the end of the block when I heard the footsteps behind me.

"Hey, loser girl."

I started to sweat and could feel the red spots bloom on my face. When I turned around, Linda was standing so close, I could smell her breath. Her drug and alcohol treatment hadn't been very successful, judging from the smell and her bloodshot blue eyes. Up close Linda was just this feather-haired, acid-washed little demon. It was amazing how scary someone that small could be.

I said another little prayer that she wouldn't do anything to me in public.

Kevin and Jack stood behind her, beside themselves with excitement at the prospect of violence. They said I was going to die. I remember thinking that it was just my luck to get killed after I finally got my hair together. I felt a bit out-of-body-ish as Linda started in on her routine.

"Hey, you little bitch. Where you been hiding? Your mommy's not going to save you this time."

Kevin and Jack stood on either side of her with their

arms folded. Once in a while Kevin said, "Yeah, bitch" or "Ha ha." Jack just stood looking angry.

I felt like I might throw up and wondered if that was a recognized self-defense technique. I just stood, knees locked, hoping not to keel over.

Linda shoved me by the shoulders. I don't know what kind of spineless sissy I am, but I didn't even put my arms up or try to protect myself at all.

"Look, the stupid bitch won't even hit me."

Shove.

"What are you supposed to be, anyway? Still think you're a gremlin?"

At this Kevin and Jack burst into high-pitched peals of nervous laughter.

"You look even stupider than you did in first grade. You're so ugly. I'll wipe that look off your face."

Then she slapped me. I couldn't believe it. It was a shocking feeling. The realization hit me that I was going to get beaten up—not just my psychological person, but my actual physical person was going to get it this time. Then a flurry of crazy blows came at me from all directions, and every one seemed to connect with my face. It didn't feel like my face, though—it felt like someone else's. I could hear her fist connecting with my head from what sounded like a great distance. And that useless pair of flailing arms didn't belong to me either. Good thing too, because if they had, I would have been very disappointed in them. My big rubber lips flapped around and my head snapped back and forth as she hit me. How did she get so fast? Were there any boxing scouts in the crowd? I was being beaten to death. Help.

And then it stopped.

When I looked up, Linda was being held by the Tragic Hot Dog Guy. He's a small man, but he somehow seemed to be holding her off the ground, probably to try to avoid her wildly kicking legs.

The Tragic Hot Dog Guy is the logger-turned-hot-dog-stand-entrepreneur failure who trundles his cart around downtown Smithers searching in vain for customers. He's always trying different marketing schemes. At one point he was giving out little chunks of hot dog and bun as samples. People just about run away when he comes at them with the little piece of mechanically separated meat in a Wonder Bread bun clutched in his plastic gloved hand. Then he gets offended and turns back to his hot dog cart, muttering and shaking his head. He always perks up and gets this awful, hopeful look in his eye whenever some out-of-towner buys one of his on-sale hot dogs. He's my favorite downtown merchant, although even I have to admit that he probably would have had an easier time if he'd stayed in the bush rather than following his dream of having his own business.

Thank God he was around, because if he hadn't been, Linda might have kept doing a Muhammad Ali on me until I was permanently damaged. When he pulled her off, I guess I was crying or whatever, because my face was wet and I could barely see. The salt from my tears was burning the cut on my lip. When I went to wipe my eyes, my hand came away covered in blood. Then I went hysterical—my eye had been cut! Man. Just like in *Rocky*. If I had a handler, this is where I would get him to cut my swollen eyelid open so I could finish the fight.

I peered around for my handler, you know, disoriented, and then realized that I was just a nice young girl having the shit kicked out of me by a nut job in feathered hair.

I guess I started bleating about my cut eye and everything, because Kevin and Jack told me to shut up. "It's just your nose, stupid." "Oh man, her face is all snotty too." "Gross."

Then the Hot Dog Guy, still holding Mad Dog Linda, told me to "get on home." Just like in the movies. There was a part of me that didn't want to leave until psycho girl had gotten it out of her system. I mean, I was pretty beat up and crying and everything, but I hoped that being held by a hot dog salesman didn't confuse her into thinking she hadn't beaten the crap out of me already.

The boys were agitated. When I walked past them, they looked at my teary, bloody, snot-smeared face with disgust. I was a car wreck of a person. Jack even looked kind of upset.

"I told ya. You shoulda listened to me. I told ya she was going to get ya," he repeated as I walked past, until Kevin hissed at him, "Shut up, man. Let's go."

By the time I walked up the hill and into our driveway, I had a huge headache. My body was wracked with pain. I was shaking like crazy, a hundred times worse than that time Linda hit me with the rock and cut my scalp, even though there was way more blood that time. Mom wasn't home yet, Dad was in the basement, and MacGregor was out somewhere. I went into the bathroom to clean up, or at least that's what I meant to do. But then I looked in the mirror and became totally fascinated. It was amazing how beat up my face looked with all the blood and stuff on it.

I stared in the mirror for a while and decided, drama queen that I am, that someone should see me like this before I cleaned up. I wondered what kind of reaction I could get out of my mom and dad. Would they take vigilante action? Head on down to the local Royal Canadian Mounted Police detachment and demand Linda's head on a plate? Maybe they would pile in the car with shotguns at the ready, MacGregor holding up the rear with a big fish net, and hunt Linda down to avenge the wrong done our clan. Or maybe we could all put on our gang colors and jump into the low rider and go ice the bitch who messed with our posse. All these scenarios made me feel so much better that the thumping pain in my head and face hardly mattered.

I was sitting on the toilet cooking up revenge fantasies when I heard my mom come in the front door, call down to Dad, and greet MacGregor. It was time for my grand entrance.

I waited until I was sure they were all in the kitchen. I paused to get the right sort of look happening before I went in. I was trying to strike a pose somewhere between a tough-yet-undefeated Billy Jack and the deformed appeal of the Elephant Man. I made sure to stagger a little bit and keep my eyes unfocused (to show how in shock I was). Then I walked into the kitchen.

It was pretty gratifying when all the conversation stopped. I mean, I don't think they were really talking too much at the time or anything, but I know they would have stopped if they had been. My father looked at me and said with real feeling, "Jesus H. Christ."

My mom, less interestingly, started crying right away. It was kind of a weird type of crying. Low, muffled sobs that weren't really directed at anybody. She put the back of her hand up to her eyes, just like a little kid who's really bawling and heartbroken, the way kids get. It was awful, actually. Not at all what I had hoped for. She looked like someone had really hurt her. And worse, when I focused a bit to look at MacGregor, he was crying too. That wasn't at all what I had in mind. He was small and teary and upset.

Oh man. This was a bad idea. And I thought it would be so fun.

I just stood there like a idiot until my dad walked over and said, "Let's go get you cleaned up." We walked out of the kitchen, where Mom and MacGregor were still crying. Dad didn't really say much. He sat me down on the toilet, took a facecloth, and started wiping the blood off my face. I don't think I have ever felt that sad in my life. I couldn't believe how defeated my dad looked. He obviously didn't know what to say.

Underneath the crusted blood I had a fat, split lip and

a puffy, beginning-to-go-black eye, and my nose was sort of swollen looking. I couldn't help thinking about that rerun of *The Dukes of Hazzard* I saw, where Daisy Duke got into a fistfight with another Southern babe wearing jean cut-offs. Old Daisy walked away with only a bit of a scratch on her cheek. It practically looked like a beauty mark. I am so much more real. I look like a monster.

I don't think Dad appreciated the authenticity of my wounds, but I kind of liked them because usually most of my problems are in my head. I suppose I can understand how a beaten face could be upsetting for a parent, though. The satisfaction I felt was not something they could be expected to understand.

After Dad washed the crud off my face, we went back into the kitchen, where Mom was making dinner. MacGregor sat at the table. My mom tried to work herself up to the subject of my face.

"Alice," she began.

"I don't want to talk about it."

"We have to talk about it."

It was cruel, I know, but I said it anyway.

"Aren't you the same person who fired me today?"

My dad looked over at my mom, surprised.

"I didn't . . ." Her face crumpled.

"Just leave me alone. There's nothing anyone can do. You'll just make it worse."

I was about to go on because suddenly I was in a rage at my mom, at my dad, at this whole stupid town. And then I saw MacGregor's face.

"Never mind," I said. "We can talk about it tomorrow. I just want to go to bed."

I didn't come out of my room all night. Mom put a plate of her version of comfort food, whole wheat macaroni and some kind of cheese substitute, just inside my door.

I slept and thought about the fight and the feeling of being hit. I also thought about my misunderstoodness showing, and looked forward to showing people outside my family.

This is going to require major modifications to my Life Goals list. For number 2, Increase contact with people outside of immediate family, I wonder if my face with Linda's fist counts. As for number 7, this definitely counts as a new look. Unfortunately it is back to being mostly sad.

JUST FINE, THANKS

August 27
Mom and Dad asked me this morning whether I wanted to go to counseling today. They said they would understand if I didn't. They looked nervous.

"Just let me handle it," I said, in my best heroic but fragile voice.

My face really looks terrible now. Swollen, blue, puffy—I'm pretty pale to begin with, and my short hair shows off my war wounds well. As I walked to the

Transition Center, I could see the people driving by do a double take when they saw my face.

I imagined them thinking I was a battered child or girlfriend or something. The air should have been filled with the sound of bagpipes.

I made sure to walk past the North Star Café so all the gossips having their morning coffee could get a good look at me. It was too early for Linda or Kevin or Jack to be out, so I figured I was safe. I wished school had already started so I could make a big entrance there too.

Even though I hadn't shown any admirable qualities, like heroism or courage or anything, during the beating, the suggestion of violence was a major draw for the Teens in Transition waiting to google at Bob. People were interested in my wounds. Some of the girls at the club revealed that they are actually aware of my existence. A few misunderstood and overly sensitive girls tried to express concern, and I did my mute-and-miserable impersonation, hoping to evoke more pity. Violet the Victim, who talks nonstop to whoever will listen, but not usually to me, walked over and nodded knowingly, like her suspicions had just been confirmed.

"People are animals," she informed me, like the revelation would come as some big surprise to me. "They always go after us sensitive ones," she continued. Then she asked if I was interested in starting up a watercolor painting club with her. I shook my head.

"I don't actually draw. Or, uh, paint."

"But you're an artist, right?" she asked, as if the answer

was obvious. I shrugged. Maybe I was. Maybe I was a per-formance artist who specialized in getting beaten up in public.

"Because they always go for us artists," finished Violet, before sighing off to consider more injustice.

Then Llona came over. She and Jim Martino are the official couple at the Teens in Transition Club. The neck-ing and lap sitting give it away. Today Llona was alone. She looked strangely incomplete.

"That totally sucks," she said, indicating my face with a wave of her hand. Or maybe she was indicating all of me.

Stumped for more conversation, she closed her mouth and rocked onto her heels a few times.

"I can talk to Jim for you," she offered finally.

God no.

"No, that's fine. Really."

"Bob said you're coming to the Alternative, eh?"

I nodded, surprised that she knew.

"Me and Jim. We go there. We'll keep an eye out for you."

She gave me another sympathetic look and walked away.

I was stunned, and for a second I thought I was going to cry. Then Single Mother/Peer Counselor walked over and asked if there was anything she could do. And that time I did cry a bit. But I pulled it together when it was my turn to go in and see Bob. It's a good thing, too, because as soon as I walked into his office and he saw my beat-up face, he started to come apart.

"Oh geez," he whispered after I sat down. "Oh man. Wow."

I kept my eyes on the floor (but not so far down that I couldn't check out his reactions).

"That's really heavy," he said. "Do you want to talk about it? I mean, of course, we are going to ... possibly should ... We have to take a look at ... how?"

It dawned on me that Death Lord Bob might not ever recover his confidence as a therapist if I stonewalled him on my beat-up face. It's not that I think Bob is a good counselor or anything, but I don't want to be responsible for his failure. I can't handle another Mrs. F. on my conscience. So I told him what happened, skipping the bit about getting fired and making it all sound like it was no big deal, like I get into fistfights pretty often and everything.

Bob was really upset. His whisper sounded dangerously strained, and I wasn't sure what I could say that would make him feel better. In fact, he started to tear up a bit, and I didn't know what to do for him.

"I'm okay, Bob." He was sucking the pleasure out of the whole thing.

I reassured him that I am actually quite inherently violent and that this didn't really mean anything or deter me from wanting to go back to school. By the end of the session, I'd gotten him calmed down. It was so exhausting that I could barely even enjoy the walk home with everyone staring at my face.

Later

Officer Ross came over tonight. My parents called him. Or maybe Bob did. Just what I need. Another helping professional. Officer Ross asked me if I wanted to press charges. He asked who had assaulted me. I'm no *Law and Order* hard case or anything, but I didn't answer him. He asked my parents to leave the room so he could talk to me alone.

"Look, Alice, I know who beat you up." Officer Ross coughed softly and cleared his throat. "But for us to do anything, you're going to have to help out."

"It's fine."

"Your parents don't think so."

Next the mayor would be over here to offer his condolences. At this rate we might be able to get the whole town council involved in my situation.

"I think it's over now."

"I can go speak to Linda's parents."

I thought of her face that time in first grade when her dad pulled her out of the office.

"No. It's fine. Really."

Relief passed over his face. "I know it's no consolation." He paused. "But Linda's situation . . . it's not good."

"I guess I know that."

Officer Ross nodded. He looked awkward, too big and uniformed for our kitchen, our house. He got heavily to his feet and handed me his card.

"Give me a call, eh? If you want to talk."

My parents walked him out and stood talking to him by his car. I watched from the kitchen window.

Later, I heard them fighting.

"Diane, we are going to have to pick up the slack. Make allowances."

"What am I supposed to do? Quit my job?"

"I'm just saying."

"Yeah. Yeah. Fine. You're just saying. School is less than a week away. I don't think I can go through that again."

I put on my headphones so I didn't have to listen to anymore.

Before bed my dad knocked on my door and asked if he could come in.

"Your mother and I have been talking. Maybe this isn't the right time for you to go back to school."

"It's fine."

"Well, maybe we should send you to school some-where else. We can come up with the money."

"It's fine. Honestly. I want to go here. In Smithers. It's all set."

Ten minutes later my mother came in and asked me the same questions in different words. No way I'm going to let Linda keep me from going back. I've got a commitment to Bob and I'm going to keep it.

August 29

I got a letter from Aubrey this morning. He apologized for how he had treated me and said he hoped he hadn't broken my heart, but there were so many demands on him that he couldn't focus on just one person. Then he went on to tell me about some girl he met at a gas station on his way back to Prince George.

Apparently he had a very deep discussion at the pump with this girl and now he's going back to see her. She and her family are the only people in the town, which basically just consists of the gas station. I wonder where that poor family is going to go when Aubrey has been talking for ten hours straight. Maybe they can sneak out and stow away in the back of a semi trailer or something. Either that or they can run away and hide in the bush and forage around for berries and roots until Aubrey decides he can't focus his energies on just one person.

By the end of today my bruises started to fade. I am pretty attached to them, so I snuck into the bathroom and doctored them up with some of my mom's makeup. Nothing too obvious, just a bit of blue eye shadow and some black eyeliner smudged around. With the touch-up the bruises look just as bad as they did right after I got them. If not worse. It's a bit of an art to accentuate bruises.

Thank God my mother's makeup collection, which dates back to disco, runs to the special-effects colors. I wish the dark-green eye shadow didn't have so much glitter in it, though. The sparkles are a dead giveaway.

I suppose I could let my face heal, but I've been having such a good time with it, I'm not ready for it to end. What kind of bizarre need is this desire of mine to look like roadkill? I bet it's just a natural reaction to the sicknesses in our society that I am particularly sensitive to. Also, all the sympathy and attention are nice. MacGregor lent me his latest issue of *National Geographic* and told me I could keep his copy of Gerald Durrell's *My Family and Other Animals*. Mom has made semi-unhealthy food for the past three nights. She even bought white bread for my lunch. Dad said that my "desire to join the Wonder Bread nation is sheer perversity," but I noticed that he packed away half a loaf with peanut butter and jam.

Bob said we are all nervous, with me going back to school and everything. He said he's barely sleeping at night and is "having trouble with food." I'm not sure if that means an eating disorder or just anxiety. With all these people worrying on my behalf, I'm starting to feel like my own concern is a little redundant.

September 1
Oh man, what a horrible weekend. I got caught with my false bruises during a MacLeod Family Weepathon. We were sitting around in the living room watching a natural-

ist show about wildebeests that MacGregor had wanted to see. One of the baby beests wasn't a very fast runner, and he ended up getting eaten by some hyenas. It was pretty harrowing to watch, expecially since I could relate to that little wildebeest. Plus they showed the killing and eating part in what I thought was unnecessary detail.

Of course, it was very emotional and everything, and definitely too much for our little family. Mom cried openly (not surprising), Dad and MacGregor did the choked-up, breathing-hard thing and, to my embarrassment, I had the tears flowing freely.

So we were all sitting around in the living room, eating popcorn and crying and watching the poor wildebeest mom mooing and acting bewildered, when Dad happened to look over at me.

"What's that on your face?" he asked.

"What do you mean?" was my quick-witted reply.

"That black stuff all over your cheeks . . . are your bruises running?"

My mother, wiping away her tears, said in this horrified voice, "Are you putting makeup on your bruises? Is that what I've been looking at all week?"

My parents were never going to understand why I liked the way my face looked. Besides, everybody was already a little overwrought with the wildebeest thing and all, so I lied.

"Actually, I wanted to start wearing makeup. School's starting tomorrow and I thought if I looked better, I might, you know, get along better."

It was shameless, I admit. But it worked.

Mom, who had been working herself up into an outrage, melted and got all tender and supportive. "Oh, honey. If you want to wear makeup, you should learn how to put it on. And probably it's best to wait until your face is better."

I assured her that I knew how to apply it, that it just looked strange because of the bruises. There was no way I was going to have my mother show me how to put it on. She only wore makeup for that short time in the seventies. I wasn't born yet, but I've seen pictures.

So now I have to try to put the damn stuff on where it's supposed to go. So much for my career in special effects.

Between the tragic nature documentaries and my return to school tomorrow, my parents are a mess. They are wandering around like ghosts, murmuring quietly to themselves and each other, pacing up and down the hallway and into the kitchen. MacGregor's the only one who has any faith.

He asked if I wanted to walk together tomorrow. I told him no. It could be dangerous and I don't want him becoming collateral damage, as they say in military circles.

TURN LEFT AT MIDDLE EARTH

September 2
I woke up at five o'clock so I'd have enough time to put on my makeup. I found this beauty magazine from 1984 in the

117

basement and got some tips from it. I figured retro makeup would best suit my overall look. I'm coming from different decades and everything, but at least it's all from the past.

Mom's makeup was extremely old and crusty. I wonder if it's possible to get poisoned through your facial skin. I just hope I don't get salmonella or something. The magazine suggested heating the eyeliner to get it to go on evenly, so I held it up close to the old pink-handled curling iron, the one we can't use on real hair since I tried to use it on Barbie and her plastic hair melted all over the barrel. I drew the softened liner all around my eyes—outside my top lashes and inside my bottom ones, and around in the inside corner of my eye. Boy, what a difference! The eyeliner was nice and black, and although it didn't actually make my eyes look any bigger—in fact they actually looked sort of smaller—it sure drew attention to them.

Then I put some of that glittery green eye shadow on top of my eyelids, pink blusher on my cheeks (which went on a little bit clumpy because it wasn't meltable—I know because I tried), and lots of pink lip gloss.

I couldn't wear the mascara because it had dried up into powder.

The makeup really made a huge difference. It was almost like wearing a disguise. A very colorful disguise. I hardly looked fearful for my life at all.

My parents, on the other hand, looked quite rough this morning. Like they hadn't slept at all. When they saw me and I asked what they thought of my eighties makeover, my mom's face froze. Dad squeezed her hand, and they both forced their mouths into smiles and nodded.

Before I left, Mom told me to call if I wanted or needed anything. Dad said he could stop by and take me out for lunch if I wanted.

"It's fine. Don't worry," I said, thinking if I sounded exasperated they might ease up.

"Have a good day," they whispered in a hoarse duet as I walked out the door in my Italian housedress and nurse shoes, Flintstones lunch bucket in hand.

MacGregor caught up with me before I'd made it to the end of the block.

"It's okay, Mac. I can make it to school on my own."

"It's on my way," he said, even though we both knew it wasn't. The high school and the Alternative are in the opposite direction from Muheim Elementary.

We arrived and I could see that the Alternative school is a portable that hunches up alongside the regular high school. The two buildings are supposed to be a sort of separate-but-equal approach to education. I assume we are segregated from the regular students due to emotional and social issues and, in my case, problems related to attempts at homeschooling. Rumor has it that things like attendance are lax, probably because school officials think we are too far gone to keep regular hours. How many classes we take in the regular school seems to depend on how disruptive we are, i.e., do we set fires or just dress funny? Being bright but socially retarded, and mainly just a danger to myself, I'll have some choice in the matter. To be honest, one or two classes with the supposed normal people seems like more than enough.

MacGregor stood and waved as I went inside. I had to try several doors before I found one that was open.

I'm in the washroom right now. There doesn't seem to be anyone else here yet except the janitor. So far, so good.

Later

I'd been instructed to go into the high school so the guidance counselor could show me around. Ms. Dean, the guidance counselor, a seemingly unflappable woman in an iron-gray crew cut and big shoes, met me at the office. We were going to tour the regular school before she took me next door to the Alternative. She informed me that I'll be taking gym as well as English in the regular school. Everything else will be in the Alternative. As the halls began to fill, I had to fight off the urge to cling to her leg. Ms. Dean moved like a tank through the crowds of kids and teachers, all yelling and talking. I bet no prison guard out in the general population has ever been more freaked out than me. Any second I was going to end up with a shiv in my back. Ms. Dean seemed to sense my concern, because when she left me outside the gym, she told me that I would be fine. It sounded like a direct order, and for some reason it made me feel a lot better.

Gym class involved meeting a very frail teacher who had us play a rousing game of Name That Equipment. We worked in teams, and all the good spellers got picked first. Then we signed liability waivers and went over the phys-ed attire regulations: no thongs outside leotards, no Speedos, no halter tops, no cropped T-shirts, and no shorts so short that underwear could be seen from below. I will be dropping gym at the first opportunity.

During class the underutilized jock girls made it clear, in a bored way, that they hated the way I looked. Not sur-prising, considering that they all seemed pretty invested in the whole sportswear thing—everything they wore was littered with that swoosh symbol. They are probably worried that if people start recycling stretch wear from the seventies and housedresses from the fifties, there won't be enough marketing dollars left for sponsorship deals when they hit the big time in Large Lumbering Girls' Lacrosse or whatever. One of the more extroverted jock girls, who is clearly blessed with a winning personal-ity, informed me that this wasn't a retirement home and asked why I was wearing an old lady's dress. A couple of her friends cleverly pointed out that I was early for Halloween. It's nice to know that those sorts of com-ments don't have the power over me they did back in first grade.

My walk through the hall to English class was instruc-tive. I was able to pick out several social subcategories and make cultural observations about them. For instance, I doubt the head banger/rockers will be inviting me to join their posse any time soon. It's sort of odd that people who wear white boots and perm their hair as a timeless fashion statement don't like my retro look. They all laughed when I walked by them in the hallway, whinnying "nice makeup" and "nice clothes." I found their attitude to my makeup strange given the war paint they had on. I guess the difference is that their makeup is heavy (like mine), but very artfully applied (unlike mine). They all seemed to be wearing foundation a good two shades lighter than their actual skin, with a good strong dividing line between the chin and the neck, and dark lip liner with really pale lipstick inside, blue eyeliner, and at least three coats of mascara.

My makeup doesn't have the practiced look theirs does. It has more of that first-time-at-the-dried-up-makeup-in-the-second-drawer-in-the-bathroom look. Even so, they didn't have to get so mean and call me a freak. I mean, we all have goobers in the corner of our eyes by lunchtime, right?

I didn't get any reaction at all from the longhairs. Far as I could tell, they were all too busy playing Hacky Sack, handing out flyers for the free lunch program, and fundraising to send themselves and a few tons of tie-dyed clothing over to the unsuspecting poor in Latin America to notice or comment on me.

I know from my reading that every school has a popular group, but I haven't yet identified them. It would be helpful if they would wear name tags, so I would know who to envy and be intimidated by.

English class had an interesting mix of students. And the teacher looked like a science fiction/fantasy fan who might be familiar with *The Lord of the Rings*. She had on knee-high boots, a tight, Federation-style tunic dress, and a newly invented hairstyle. I made a mental note to bring my copy of *Fellowship* to the next class so we can bond over shared literary tastes. I'll just have to hope she doesn't want to talk about anything past the Prologue.

She seemed friendly enough, but very intense. She dispensed with the banter in just over a minute and then started reading a story by the guy who supposedly predicted the Internet. Bingo! I was right. She *is* a sci-fi fan. And a feminist. Our first reading assignment is *The Handmaid's Tale*. Life Goals-wise, this woman and I are really in sync.

I noticed another group in the class—the nice, quiet people. They were the ones the teacher called on. I plan to watch out for them. They're probably all so nice and quiet because they aren't too sure about the whole fitting-in thing—something I'd imagine they are desperate to do. My homeschooled hostility and outrageous personal esthetic will probably be threatening to their whole get-along-at-all-costs worldview. It would be those quiet ones who'd kick you when you're down, I bet. Or make the nastiest comments (which they've had time to think up in all that silence).

I was called to the office just as class was ending. The secretary handed me a sealed envelope.

Inside was a note from my dad. He was waiting outside in the car. He'd driven by a couple of times but hadn't seen anything "untoward" going on. My father is so mental. I found him hunched down in the Wonderwagon in the teachers' parking lot.

He rolled down the window and cautiously poked his face out.

"Dad, it's fine."

"So it's okay then?"

"God, yes."

He wanted to ask a hundred questions. I could see them spinning behind his eyes. But he held back.

"I'll just wait here another minute," he said. "Just another few minutes. Then I'll go let your mother know how it's going."

I went back to the office so Ms. Dean could take me over to the Alternative. We were just leaving when Bob rushed in, black hair wild.

"I'm here, I'm here," he panted.

Ms. Dean looked at him steadily.

"I was just taking Alice over to the Alternative."

"Excellent. Excellent," gasped Bob, bent over with hands on knees as he struggled to catch his breath.

Ms. Dean waited for Bob to recover. "Are you going to be all right?"

"Oh. Yes. No problem. No problem."

Bob had turned into Mr. Say It Two Times. Interesting.

"You're going to come with us then?" Ms. Dean asked Bob.

"I thought I'd oversee. I mean, you know, come along."

Ms. Dean sort of smiled and rolled her eyes. "Okay then."

"See, this isn't so bad," Bob counseled me, looking over with what was probably supposed to be a smile, that fled off his face, leaving a look of horror in its place.

"Your face," he choked. "It's—"

"It's eighties," Ms. Dean stated. "All the rage this year. Depeche Mode. Culture Club. Black lipstick. It's all back."

"Really?" Bob looked at her with pleading eyes.

"Oh yeah. Alice is right with the program, makeup-wise."

Bob exhaled slowly and nodded.

Ms. Dean walked ahead of us, and Bob turned to me again.

"Well," he stage-whispered, "how's it going?"

I shrugged. "Okay. I guess."

"So everything's okay?"

"Yeah. It's fine."

"Good." He straightened a bit and looked past me into the crowded foyer. He nodded to himself. "Good."

I could tell right off that the Alternative school is supposed to be really unauthoritarian and everything. The teachers seemed nice but a bit too social-workerish. Take Mr. Richards, for example. He's one of those fleece-wearing outdoorsy people who look so healthy that they don't even look real. He looks like he should have something more adventurous to do with his life than teach misfits, like maybe he should be heli-skiing or hang gliding in the Andes. Maybe he does that stuff on weekends with some freckled, braided bombshell. But during the day Mr. Richards is sensitivity personified.

When we walked in, he and Bob greeted each other like they went way back, or at least back to the conference on conflict resolution techniques for youth workers they met at last month.

"Bob!" Mr. Richards made no effort to hide his enthusiasm.

"Doug!"

They gave each other hearty heterosexual hugs, men at ease with themselves and their masculinity.

They backslapped each other a few times and smiled broadly, looking each other right in the eyes. Finally, Ms. Dean cleared her throat.

"Right." Bob stepped back. "Doug, I'd like you to meet Alice MacLeod. The new student I mentioned would be joining you."

"Great!" Doug turned to me. "You can call me Doug. Or Mr. Richards. Whichever you prefer."

I nodded, not nearly as comfortable with myself as Bob and Mr. Richards were.

Another teacher, with a zodiac chart on her oversized T-shirt, came over.

There was a pause, and finally Ms. Dean introduced her.

"And this is Ms. Swinke."

"Right," Mr. Richards agreed, without enthusiasm.

"Hello, Alice." The woman's voice was extremely

gentle, as though she was speaking to someone about to jump off a ten-story ledge.

"Hi."

With effort, Ms. Dean finally dragged Bob away, and Mr. Richards and Ms. Swinke invited me to sit down. Looking around, I would have described the crowd as more motley than eclectic. It was a lot like the Teens in Transition Club, only with more boys. There wasn't even one athlete I could see, unless some of the kids competed in the Running from the Cops 500-meter event. I felt embarrassingly at home. I recognized several people from the Teen Club, including Violet and Llona and Jim.

We were just starting Life Skills class when in walked Kevin and Jack. Oh my God! Why hadn't I realized that they would be in the Alternative? I had counted on them being kicked out by now, but they must not be as hardcore as Linda. I hadn't seen them since the fight. I considered screaming and running to hide behind Mr. Richards but decided against it. That is exactly what everyone would expect from a home-based learner. I forced myself to stay seated.

The boys sat down at my table. There are no individual desks at the Alternative, probably because our antisocial tendencies are too pronounced already. Instead they make us sit at tables for four, which supposedly encourages group interaction and is handy for Family Studies, where we pretend we are teen parents trying to cope with the stress of a baby, played in our class by a hard-boiled egg instead of the raw one they apparently get in the regular school. Oddly enough, the Life Skills topic of the day was violence, where and why it happens, and what we can do about it. Mr. Richards asked us whether we had ever seen or experienced violence. Violet the Victim started in with a horror story. Jim started flexing his biceps and talking about the time he kicked "that bastard Anthony Donatello's ass." Llona looked at him with big glazed doughnut eyes while he mimicked stomping Anthony's head. Mr. Richards was eating it up. He seemed to love all this slice of life among the Alternative school behavior cases. Kevin had been shooting me the meaningful stare of death since he and Jack sat down. Jack looked down at his desk. When Mr. Richards sensed some of the more sensitive students about to get triggered, he stopped Jim's flexing and grunting.

Mr. Richards was launching into a feel-good empowerment lecture when Kevin put up his hand to ask a question.

"Mr. Richards, if you knew that someone was going to get beat up, maybe even killed, should you tell them? Because someone in this class is in a lot of danger."

Mr. Richards put an exaggeratedly puzzled and concerned look on his face, like he was coming face to face with inner-city gang violence and limited-opportunity structure or something.

"Yeah, sir. Someone in this class is going to get stomped. I'm not threatening or anything. It's not like I hope it happens, 'cause, like, I don't. I hate violence, man."

"Well, Kevin. I'm glad you told us that. You know, it's important that everyone in this class feel safe. I hope that if anyone is in trouble, they will come see me or one of the other teachers."

Kevin whispered over to me, "Hey, ugly. You better go see him. Before Linda kills you and your psycho mother. You were just lucky that hot dog guy stopped her from erasing your map the last time. Linda don't forget stuff like that."

His threat was interrupted by Violet, who trilled, "Violence against artists! Violence against artists!" in a voice so high-pitched that dogs from all over town probably headed for the classroom.

Everyone in the class turned. They followed her eyes to look at me, frozen at the table.

Llona elbowed Jim, who, with effort, put up his muscle-bound arm.

"Nobody's touching nobody in this class. Not even if they dress funny and shit."

Kevin looked around, surprised and angry.

"Screw this action. Mr. R., man, I gotta go to the can."

Mr. Richards nodded, distracted by the diagram of cycles of violence he was drawing on the board.

"Go ahead, Kevin."

Kevin got up and looked down expectantly at Jack. Jack shrugged slightly and stayed seated.

Kevin growled a short, sharp swear word and stomped out.

Mr. Richards was so busy radiating compassion and understanding that he didn't notice any of it.

I guess all in all it was an okay first day. It sure could have been worse. I'm a pariah at the regular school and an object of pity at the special school, but I'm still in one piece and that's the main thing.

September 3
It turns out that I am allergic to really old makeup. My whole face is covered with scaly red blotches. Not only that, but apparently you aren't supposed to put eyeliner over that tiny hole at the inside corner of your eye. I did, and now one of my tear ducts is blocked and swollen to pea size and very sore. It's amazing, but I actually look more loathsome than I did right after the beating.

Mom has gone and made an appointment for me with some beautician friend of hers so I can learn how to put makeup on properly. I guess she thinks that the early eighties style isn't working. She said she would buy me new makeup after my "makeover." For such a granola, my mother is pretty into this whole face-paint thing. I can't even speculate on what that means—I have a feeling, though, that it's none too complimentary to me.

Her esthetician friend had better not be as flamingly incompetent as Irma. I've been through a lot lately. I'm too fragile to deal with another disaster.

I discovered something about high school today. A person can go from New and Noteworthy to Completely Invisible in just one day. Not one person in the regular school or the Alternative commented on my fashion statement, even though I wore completely different clothes than yesterday. Apparently a person has to dress like a hobbit to stay in the public eye for any length of time. Fine with me.

In Life Skills class today, when Mr. Richards turned his back to draw a diagram of the cycle of failure for young people, Kevin leaned over to me and whispered, "Hey, you little hose. Linda isn't done with you yet."

Jack giggled uneasily and pulled on his pot-leaf earring. Nobody else heard.

It could have been worse. One of them could have asked me out.

At the end of class Mr. Richards and Ms. Swinke took me into their office. I guess Mr. Richards had noticed Kevin threatening me yesterday. Either that or he realized that anyone who looks as alternative as me is probably going to experience some kind of violent opposition from mediocre minds. Or Bob's been breaking his confidentiality agreement.

The Alternative school teachers' staff room-counseling office is enough to make even the toughest POW crack, never mind someone like me who's actually quite cowardly. I don't know what the offices for regular teachers are like, but they put the Alternative teachers in what looks like a boiler room. It's littered with private-life-of-teachers stuff everywhere—coffee cups with their first names and teacher jokes on them, reading materials—embarrassing stuff like that. I don't see how it is possible to be effectively counseled in a room filled with personal possessions from teachers' real lives. I've been in school for only two days, and even I know that most kids wish the teachers weren't allowed out of the school at all. Sort of like I wish my parents couldn't leave the house. It's too bad adults can't be kept in a closet somewhere until they are needed. Adult private lives are embarrassing for us and should be for them.

Mr. Richards and Ms. Swinke told me they'd been "looking into my situation" and wanted to know how they could help. They asked how my mother and I were "holding up." They wanted to know if I'd heard from "Mrs. Freison since she went away." On and on it went. They'd heard that I had "a tough time this summer." I don't know whether I was supposed to have some kind of emotional meltdown and confess all, just because I was so grateful they had taken the time to gossip about me. Besides, I don't know what they figured they were going to do about my problems. Maybe send me over to the neighboring town with all new ID, and a false nose and glasses so I could make a new start. Mr. Richards hit eleven on the sincerity scale when he expressed his concern and desire to help. I was all demure and whispered selflessly about not wanting to cause any trouble.

If Mr. Richards (Doug) is painfully sincere, Ms. Swinke is a thousand times worse. She supposedly teaches history and science, but she's always trying to work the fact that she's a Wiccan into the conversation. Witch or not, she seems exactly like my mom's power-to-the-goddess, hand-me-that-sage-I-want-to-appropriate-some-rituals friends. Today in class Ms. Swinke gave us a talk about keeping "our overwhelming negativity contained." She thinks that the release of negative energy makes it hard for the "sensitive energies" in the class to open up. Ms. Swinke radiates a few negative vibes herself. Like the other New Agers I've met, she seems really angry about something, even though she puts on a big show about how peaceful and serene she is. I wouldn't be surprised to hear about a few New Agers going postal–gunning down everyone in their yoga center or whatever. Ms. Swinke could be the first. She certainly seems tightly wound enough.

She tried to Oprah me with some personal advice. "You know, Alice, I respect individuality and personal fashion statements as much as the next person, but yours, well . . ."

Mr. Richards gave her a look. "She looks cool. Urban. The clothes are not the problem." Then he addressed me. "Don't go changing."

Ms. Swinke was offended. "Fine then, Doug. So what *is* the problem?"

"It's not clothes, Carolyn. Alice just started. It's going fine."

"Maybe it's clothes and certain behaviors in class. Like making faces when others speak."

"Come on, Carolyn. Don't you mean making faces when *you* speak? They all do that."

She turned to face Mr. Richards, who is perhaps not as sensitive as I thought. "Excuse me?"

I had to step in before they could show me more of the cracks running through their professional relationship.

"Thanks. I, um, know what you're getting at. And I appreciate it. Everything is fine."

Then Mr. Richards floundered around trying to raise

my self-esteem, and Ms. Swinke tried to unstick her sour
face before excusing herself, saying she was sure Mr.
Richards could handle the rest of the meeting.

What followed was definitely a three-points-for-effort
performance from Mr. Richards, but even he dwindled off
toward the end of the big violence-intervention talk.

"So you'll let me know if you have any problems. Or
you need any help?"

"Sure."

"Or the police. You'll contact them, if you get into
trouble."

"It's fine. I'll be fine," I lied.

He might be athletic, but Linda could take him.

Later

I think Ms. Swinke or Mr. Richards must have called a few
minutes ago. After the phone rang, my parents went into a
big huddle. Usually they are embarrassingly open, but now
they've gotten all furtive about issues to do with me. I
actually appreciate it. I hate discussing my problems. It's a
bit too much like an afternoon talk show with all the bad
grammar, cheap clothes, and name calling. It's a mark of
civilization to keep things bottled up inside.

They each made a point of stopping by my room and
asking how my day was. And word for word, they both
told me that they wanted me to "feel comfortable talking"
to them about things. Then they went for a walk together.
Dealing with me is bringing them closer together.

And I don't want to disappoint them by telling them

that I am pretty much old news at school. Nobody even notices me enough to bully me. Which is a relief. I guess.

September 5
Mom and I went to get my makeover done after school today. I don't want to look like every other eighties retread at Smithers Senior Secondary, and extremely professional model-style makeup is probably the route to go.

The makeup lady's name is Zoë, and it turns out that she is another friend of the poorly shod, sexually alternative Finn. Zoë's fashion statement is pretty much car-wreck-involving-flower-trucks. It's one of those things where you can't decide whether you're delighted or nauseated. Zoë's basement, which is where her Beautifying Studio/Salon is located, was stuffed with fake and dead flowers. There were flowers dried in bunches and hanging from the ceiling. Silk and plastic flowers thrust out of pots in every corner. Zoë herself was, mysteriously, since there was no prom in the area that I knew of, wearing a huge corsage. Even stranger was that, for a place without any fresh flowers, the salon smelled overpoweringly of roses. There was a bit of a chemical undertone to the scent, which may have been offgassing from the plastic flowers. After being in Zoë's Beautifying Salon, I know what a corpse at a low-rent funeral must feel like.

Zoë was every inch the esthetician. No part of her looked natural. Her nails were cripplingly long and pink and false, her hair was short and a startling red found nowhere in nature. Most interestingly, her face didn't appear to have any pores. I can't imagine a woman who looked less like my mother, but they seemed to be friends. Maybe that's what Mom means when she goes on about folk music having no barriers—everyone from hippies to cosmetic criminals can enjoy the tuneless sounds of folk music and consider themselves daringly artsy.

So after Zoë and Mom cooed at each other for a while, they turned to me—the project for the day. I probably did look a bit bland in that overblown basement, but who wouldn't? Zoë had me sit in a pink vinyl hairdressing chair, and pumped it up until my face was almost on a level with hers. Mom stood at the counter staring intently as Zoë began draping pieces of colored fabric around my head and shoulders, to find my "tones," she said. The colors she was using were all extremely ugly, which was a bit of a concern, as were her frequent comments on the inadequacies of my skin.

"Oh honey, you see all the green this brings out in you? See how you look sick? Well, you are definitely a sallow."

A sallow, no less! Well, lucky me. Heaven forbid I should be, like, an ivory or something. No, I have to be sallow.

"Now this one shows all your blemishes. See that there? How blotchy you look? You are definitely not some-one who can get away with this color."

And on and on it went.

I have to admit, I was surprised to find out I was a

spring. I thought I would be a dead of winter, for sure. I mean, I am temperamentally.

Having decided what season I was, she started unloading makeup from these little cases on the counter. I gag even to write it, but being made up made me feel like a princess. Not just a regular princess, but a fairy princess, you know, the type who can feel a pea under a whole stack of mattresses.

Maybe my parents stole me from a royal family somewhere and now my noble roots are starting to show. That could be why I'm so sensitive. And different. It could be the reason I don't fit in. If only there were princess positions available. I would be perfect for the job.

The princess feeling must have been coming from deep inside me, because it sure wasn't coming from the way Zoë was treating me. For a woman who looked like she didn't have any bones under her skin, she was surprisingly businesslike about applying makeup. Brisk and efficient, she smoothed on the foundation, adding a darker shade on the sides of my "no need to call attention to our defects" nose. She took aim with the eyeliner like a surgeon. She contoured my lids with shades from the row of little containers filled with complementary shadows.

Her professionalism was so reassuring, I nearly fell asleep. If I ever have an operation, I hope the doctor is as good as Zoë the esthetician.

My lips were outlined just a bit outside where they actually ended and filled in with two types of lipstick. The blusher and powder went on last.

When I woke up enough to look in the mirror, I was startled. I looked like one of those freak child models. It wasn't that I looked bad–I actually looked pretty attractive, in a put-together, matched-sweater-set kind of way, but I looked really old. I looked like a thirty-six-year-old first grader.

Well, I guess I didn't look quite that bad. Just sort of like I should be wearing a pair of pumps four sizes too big and a rope of pearls hanging to my knees. My old eighties unprofessional makeup kind of matched the rest of me. This new makeup didn't fit. I've noticed that makeup makes people who don't usually wear it look much older until they are about sixty; then it does the opposite and makes them look like children. The backward effect only works if someone doesn't usually wear the stuff. Grandma hardly ever puts makeup on, but when she does, she gets this look like she's been in Mr. Dressup's Tickle Trunk. It seems like the older people get, the harder it is to put on lipstick between the lines–probably because the lines start going all over the place.

I don't think the whole properly applied makeup thing is going to work for me–I'll either apply it badly or not at all. That was confirmed for me when fashion felon Finn came over and told me I looked pretty good with proper makeup rather than "painted up like a dog's breakfast." If he has anything positive to say about the new makeup, it must be pretty bad. I let Mom buy all the stuff, though. I mean, she was so into it and everything. I wouldn't have wanted to disappoint her. It was kind of like when I took piano lessons from the nuns at the Catholic school for about two weeks. Mom got all excited because she was convinced I had finally found something I liked and that I was going to become this genius child prodigy with piano-playing, super-achiever type friends and everything. I knew after a couple of lessons that I didn't like the piano much, but I kept going because the nun who taught me had this unusual smell that I wanted to identify (I do that sometimes; it's sort of a hobby). So when Mom went out and spent all her dough on a piano, I didn't try to stop her. I figured that would have been cruel. So we got the piano, and of course I didn't play it, and now we just use it for sorting coupons. Dad keeps them filed between the keys. MacGregor uses the piano instructional books for pressing leaves and stuff. Mom was pretty annoyed at me for not following through, but I don't see why. It's our nicest piece of furniture, and she had her moment of thinking I had a constructive hobby.

Oh yeah, and on the topic of not following through, I haven't forgotten about *Fellowship*. I'm on the last page of the Prologue, but other culture is currently getting in the way of my reading. Bob wanted a Life Goal update. Now that my big one is accomplished and I'm back in school, I had to give him something, so I told him about becoming a cultural critic. Being the helping professional that he is, he wanted to help, so for our last session he brought in this movie called *The Unbelievable Truth*. It was excellent and funny and about being your own person no matter what anyone thinks, and I hate to admit it, but maybe there's a reason all the girls at the Teens in Transition think Bob's great besides the fact that he has a good slouch and he looks a little French. I mean, how many counselors would allow videos during sessions? Bob let other people in to watch and someone made microwave popcorn and a social worker candidate kept the kids in the play area so even the single moms got a break. And all for me. Lucky I have such good taste. If it had been a movie for Violet, we'd probably have been watching a documentary about some head-in-the-oven artist.

NEW FRONTIERS

September 6
I am very busy. I've been trying to listen to a tape that Bob lent me so I can be more cultural. But the music, by some band called Bauhaus, is so depressing I can barely breathe. If this is what Bob listens to, no wonder he dresses like the world's gloomiest undertaker. And there are too many distractions around this house. My dad is having his poker night here. It's quite a sight to see all the least productive men in town getting together. Mom won't admit it's a poker night. She calls it a men's meeting. Some woman misheard Mom talking about it a while ago and thought she said "Mensa meeting," and now everyone thinks that

we have this gathering of geniuses at our house once a month.

Fat chance. I guess the rumor just adds to the mystique of all these men without visible means of employment. The only elite thing about Dad's poker group is their incredibly advanced responsibility-shirking techniques.

I actually prefer Dad's friends to Mom's. His are meaner and pretty funny, at least until they get too drunk. Then they're just sloppy. In fact, I probably learn more about life from sitting around listening to my dad's friends talk than I do anywhere else. It's one of the benefits of not having a peer group. I get to hear how they do things in the big leagues.

For instance, one of my main models for how to run a love life is my dad's friend Finn. He's here tonight, in his bad shoes. Finn is absolute proof that stereotypes aren't a good way to categorize people. The whole gay-man-equals-clean-handsome-and-well-dressed thing has nothing to do with Finn. He has the worst fashion sense I've ever seen, and coming from this town, that's really saying something.

It's not just the vinyl-tasseled loafers all buckled down at the heel. It's the pilled polyester dress pants, the light-blue dress shirt, and shiny green curling jacket with his name in fuzzy letters on the back that put Finn into the farthest reaches of bad taste. Oh yeah, and his perm. The man perms his own hair. There is no way MacGee does Finn's hair—it's a disgrace even Irma would be ashamed of.

Dad swears that Finn just has unfortunate-looking hair and that I'm unnecessarily shallow and judgmental. He is always pointing out how many friends and "friends" (eyebrows meaningfully inclined) Finn has, as though that is some kind of proof that Finn has decent taste and doesn't perm his hair. I say his popularity has everything to do with the fact that Finn will drink with anyone, anytime. That's a real bonus in a town where people allow nondrinking only in small children and religious fanatics.

One thing you can say about Finn is that he's honest. Once he was dating a dying man. I can't remember just what was wrong with the guy—Reginald, I think his name was—but whatever it was, it was fatal. Anyway, Reginald came to Smithers to visit after meeting Finn in a bar in Prince George. Reginald, although good-looking and terribly ill, was apparently the most annoying man.

Finn came over to our house for coffee and said in this defeated way that he didn't think it was going to work out with Reginald. I could have told him that. As my dad said at the time, it usually doesn't last with the terminally ill. After his confession Finn heaved a big sigh. Then another one.

"I don't know, you know? What am I going to do?"

Dad tried to get Finn to talk about what was wrong.

"Oh my God. I can't say it. I just can't. It's too bad. Oh, all right. I hate him."

He clapped his hand over his mouth for a moment as if to stifle his revelations.

"It's just that, you know, he's not well and everything. What kind of a monster am I?"

Dad reassured Finn that he was just expressing his feelings and told him it would do him good to get it off his chest. Of course, Dad loved it. He loves gossip, and the sicker the stories, the better he likes them.

So Finn got into it. He said that Reginald was a Pollyanna. I guess that Reginald, being sick and all, was a health nut. Personally, I don't think he could have been all that healthy, psychologically at least, if dating Finn in the last days of his life seemed like a good option.

Apparently Reginald did a lot of talking about positive energy and eating right, the sort of stuff that bores Finn to death. When the two of them went out hiking, Reginald wanted to walk the whole way, as opposed to stopping after five minutes to sit and have cocktails out of a thermos until the rest of the party came back, which is how Finn likes to hike.

The dying Reginald, with all his positive thoughts and healthy actions, was pretty much killing Finn. Reginald hardly drank at all, except for a civilized glass of wine with dinner, and during his visit he made sure that they ate vegetables with their meals and fruit for breakfast. After a couple of weeks Finn was really starting to hate him.

Not long after he confessed his dislike of his houseguest to my dad, Finn brought Reginald over to visit. Normally Finn is pretty energetic, or at least he keeps up his end of the conversation with nasty comments and snide remarks between drinks. But around Reginald he was mute and lumpish.

Reginald was a stereotypical gay man. There's no way around it, even though I'm opposed to the whole stereotyping thing. He was tall, clean-cut, handsome, well-spoken, and charming. He looked incredibly healthy. Not Finn, though. He was pale and shaking. I think all the clean living was putting him into some kind of physical crisis. Every time Reginald made some remark, usually something nice or interesting or whatever, Finn tried to rally and say something negative, but it was no use. Reginald stayed positive and happy. Finally, Finn just rolled his eyes like a sick cow whenever Reginald spoke.

They decided to go golfing after their visit and Finn hired me to caddy, even though I don't know anything about golf. I think he was afraid to be alone with Reginald. When we got to the course, Reginald refused to take a cart. Finn asked him how he expected a fifty-pound child to carry both their bags. After two holes Finn pretended that he'd forgotten something in the clubhouse and said he had to go get it. He never came back. So I had to carry his golf bag around the whole course as I followed after Reginald. It's a good thing Reginald is almost a champion golfer. If we'd gone at the rate we were when Finn was playing, it would have taken all day to get around. Anyway, by the end of the game, even though Reginald was so nice and talented and dying and everything, I knew what Finn was talking about. Reginald *was* a Pollyanna. I admire Finn's advanced hiding and shirking techniques, actually. After

Reginald's visit, I vowed to use them in my own romantic life, if I ever get one. Not long after the golf game Finn told Reginald that it was over, and Reginald went back to Prince George.

Finn's not even the most pathetic of my father's poker buddies. Marcus is also here for poker night. My mother doesn't like him because he goes out with younger women. Much younger women. He's around forty and is usually dating some girl who is around twenty. I'm not sure how he gets the girls to go out with him–he's not good-looking, or rich, or talented or anything like that. But he *is* the owner of the only taxicab in town, which is something, I guess.

Maybe the girls who go out with Marcus are just in it for the ride. Whenever he comes over for poker night, he gets calls from the girlfriend of the moment, demanding that he come and pick her up from the cabaret or gravel-pit party or wherever. They always end up having these shrill conversations where you can hear her voice squawking out of the receiver and him whining back at her. Then Marcus has to make up an excuse to the rest of the geniuses and go pick up his much younger girlfriend.

I personally think Mom has it backward about just who is being exploited in Marcus's relationships. The girls he goes out with cost him a fortune in lost business. It's almost impossible to get a cab because Marcus is always out chauffeuring his latest hot little number around while she shops. If you ask me, transit in this town would be greatly improved if Marcus got older taste in women, especially since Smithers doesn't have a bus or anything.

Kelly is the fourth player tonight. He's very quiet and cries a lot, especially when he drinks. Dad says he's sensitive. Apparently Kelly's so sensitive, he has held only one job in his adult life. He helped out at the video store for a while but got so undone by the dramas he played in the store that it was disturbing to the customers. They were just coming in for the new releases, or the latest World Wrestling Federation match or whatever, and ended up having to stay and comfort Kelly through the last half of *Terms of Endearment* or *Ordinary People*. Needless to say, the video store job didn't work out. Kelly doesn't ever have a girlfriend of his own, but he admires Marcus and seems to live vicariously through him, which is sort of terrifying and sad when you think about it.

So that's my Dad's Mensa group. Because they hardly make any money, they don't have a lot to bet with. Sometimes someone new, someone with an income, joins them. If the new guy has the poor judgment to raise the stakes so they have to match him, the geniuses go into this injured-silence routine, leaving the new guy with no idea what he did wrong. They hardly ever ask anyone new.

Anyway, they're all in the kitchen giggling like girls and making a lot of noise, and I can't concentrate on my book or the incredibly grim stylings of Bauhaus. I don't really have anything else to concentrate on. I'm underwhelmed by the bustle of life. Talk about paralysis from

information overload, only I guess in my case it's backward—paralysis from lack of stimulation and living in this
dumb town. My apathy is all I have left, really. I read in
Spin magazine recently that negativity and irony and cyni-
cism are out. I'm here to say that that particular trend has
not made it to my house yet. Maybe I'll go watch the
geniuses nickel-and-dime each other to death.

September 7

No. 3. Learn to drive a car. Check! Almost dance. Check!

Last night was awesome! The Mensa players all got
drunk, and I drove them and MacGregor to the Annual
Princess Diana Memorial Service at Driftwood Hall. I now
know how to drive a car! I have been to a large Smithers
party. I could almost be considered worldly at this point.

Driftwood Hall is about twenty miles outside of town.
It's the sort of place where the Rotary and hockey clubs
hold dances and people drink till they drop. It's very
Smithers.

I can't believe my dad let me drive. I don't think he
can believe he did either. He didn't even know driving
was one of my major Life Goals! Sometimes you just can't
stop progress. Mom was out at some hippie thing, so she
wasn't there to get in the way. Finn convinced everyone
that since Diana's death was one of the most important
cultural events in our lifetime, it was our duty to remember it by going to the service. Besides, they had already
dropped the whole fifty cents they brought to the poker
game and were bored.

I'm not sure how Finn convinced Dad to let me drive everyone to Driftwood in Marcus's cab. Of course, MacGregor and I were the only sober ones, and I *am* taller than MacGregor.

Even though Finn was all for me driving, he pulled out a lot of used hockey gear—helmets and shoulder pads and everything—and made everyone put it on before getting in the car. I thought that showed a real lack of faith. Plus I had trouble seeing, because my helmet was too big and kept slipping over my eyes. So with four hulking, padded, and helmeted drunken men and one boy wearing what looked like a full-length dress styled like a hockey jersey, I lurched off for my first drive in the ancient Lincoln Continental. It was pretty stressful, what with Finn giving me orders, Dad being fatherly and supportive, Kelly weeping, and Marcus insisting that I leave the "available" light on in case we found a fare. Marcus kept reminding me to say "Ten-four, old buddy" into his CB radio, which wasn't even attached to a dispatch or anything. Only someone as committed to life experience as me could learn to drive under such conditions. I have to admit that although I could have handled it on my own, I was grateful to have MacGregor along for the ride. He was the only one paying enough attention to tell me how things worked. I had to concentrate so hard that I barely even thought about the fact that my first drive was to a place where we would be honoring the memory of someone who died in a horrible car crash. Finn brought it up a few times, but everyone ignored him.

I had the brakes and the lights figured out by the end of the driveway with only minor assistance from MacGregor. By Main Street I had the heat on high and the hazard lights working. By the highway I had discovered low gear, the windshield wipers, and the button that made the left rear window go down. We were off.

"Great, honey," said my father. To the geniuses, "You see? I told you she was bright." And back to me, "I'm very proud of you. And you'll be sure and not mention this to your mother?"

"Just pick up that receiver and say 'Ten-four, good buddy' . . . or is it old buddy? Hell, I can never remember. Never mind. Are you sure the light is lit? . . . Anyway, she put two hundred Ks on this car in the last two weeks. And not a penny in fares. Why does a twenty-year-old girl have to drive everywhere she goes? You'd think she would want to walk once in a while. You know, to keep her figure and all. . . ."

Finn complained, "Good God, it's hot in here! Was that the turnoff? Kelly, stop blubbering and fasten your seat belt. We're going like a bat out of hell. Turn! Turn! God, this must have been exactly how Di and Dodi felt in their last moments. . . ."

I got it up to 50 kilometers an hour on one straight stretch and probably could have gone faster, but MacGregor said that was probably about the right speed. Dad was very proud until he fell asleep.

There were about six or seven cars in the parking lot when we finally got to the hall. In full protective hockey gear we struggled out of the car, sweating profusely. There were a few cheap bouquets of wilted carnations sitting at the entrance. Driftwood Hall is a squat building with double doors on all four sides, probably designed for line dancers who have to be sick at a moment's notice. The crummy little bouquets looked small and sad sitting there in squalid heaps. They sent Kelly into a fit of grief. He was so out of control that Marcus and Finn had to hold him up and escort him in.

We couldn't wake up Dad, so we left him in the car. He's not as serious a drinker as the rest of the geniuses because he has a habit of passing out early. It's a blessing, really. MacGregor and I followed Finn and the others at what I hoped was enough distance that no one would think we were with them. I have enough problems without being associated with the geniuses in a social sense.

A VCR and big-screen TV were hooked up at the far end of the hall. A few tight knots of people huddled at some folding tables set up in front of the screen. The video had started, and the funeral procession was moving through the weeping crowd. The commentator was making dead-on observations like "The emotions are obviously running high here today," and "That woman in the crowd there seems to be crying quite a bit." Apparently there would be no service at the Memorial Service, just a TV rerun of Diana's funeral.

Everyone was really paying attention to the screen and being very serious. A cheap pink candle burned on every table. The room itself looked about the same as when we went to my mother's friend's wedding last year, only this time there was no goat with flowers on its head wandering around. A bar at the back of the hall was staffed by a guy wearing a Royal Order of Elks fez. Every so often one of the mourners made a quick run to the bar.

Once Finn and Marcus had helped the hysterical Kelly into a seat close to the TV, they made their way to the bar, historic cultural moment taking a backseat to their need for refreshment. They attracted some hostile stares from the angry-looking types sitting at a table quite close to the TV, who looked like they were probably religious. They weren't drinking and wore a lot of pastel colors. I heard them muttering when we came in, and they turned around and glared every time someone got up to go to the bar.

I sat with MacGregor and Kelly, who was sniffling and wiping his nose on the sleeve of his hockey jersey. Our table was covered with a pile of helmets and assorted protective gear. I could see Finn leaning against the plywood opening of the bar, a jockstrap over his jeans and a neck brace cinched under his chin. Marcus wandered distractedly around in stained shoulder and shin pads looking for a phone to call his girlfriend.

So far the funeral rerun was mostly just the hearse driving through the crowd, but the announcer said they were getting close to Westminster Abbey or wherever it was they were burying the princess. Finally the hearse got to the church. Just then people started to pour into the hall. I guess the people who'd been at a nearby bush party decided it was getting cold, so they moved to the Princess

Diana Memorial. The angry religious people were beside themselves. They moved in closer to the TV screen and turned up the volume. Meanwhile some bush-party refugee backed his pickup truck up to one of the hall doors and put his stereo speakers in the back so they pointed inside.

Marcus's girlfriend arrived with a few of her friends. As soon as she saw Marcus, they started arguing. She yelled at him for following her and accused him of not letting her have her own life. He apologized and asked if she needed a ride anywhere. She told him she wanted to sit with her friends and he should let her have her space. Marcus came and sat down with us. Then I saw Jack and Kevin arrive, white-booted girlfriends in tow. It was pretty tense, even after I realized that Linda wasn't with them.

Somebody turned up AC/DC on the truck stereo so we couldn't hear the memorial video at all. There was some friendly tussling between a cowboy hat-wearing country music fan and a heavy metal fan over what music to play. The religious people were by now totally outraged, and they turned up the volume so high that the TV started to shake. I lost sight of Jack and Kevin and breathed a deep sigh of relief.

Four very drunk women in sawdust-covered lumber jackets sat down around me and MacGregor. One of them tried to kiss MacGregor, saying he reminded her of her little brother. She was distracted by her friend, who was taking bets on whether I was from "the city." It was looking like I was from the city for a while. "Oh come on,

Lorna, look at her hair! That's Vancouver hair! Five bucks and a beer says that's Vancouver hair!" But her friend pointed out that the hair might be Vancouver, but "What about the hockey jersey, eh? That's Smithers if I ever seen it."

The betting was interrupted when the debate over Garth Brooks versus AC/DC turned violent. The country fan was dragged out of the truck, which he was sneaking into in an effort to change the tape. He and the heavy metal guy started rolling around on the floor, and the lumber-jacket women, who apparently were on leave from a forestry service crew and had something to prove, saw their chance and jumped in.

Then Elton John came on TV to do his Marilyn Monroe song, which was beautiful and everything, but I figure that with Diana's wardrobe, she should probably have gotten her own song, not just one with the words changed a bit. I guess that's one of the bad things about dying suddenly. Nobody has time to come up with something good for your funeral. If I had a lot of money, like Diana did, I would have had someone write my funeral song in advance, to make sure I had my own. Your funeral is a pretty important event. You want your own song or at least your favorite song at the last party you are ever going to have.

Anyway, when Elton started the song, it was drowned out by all the grunting from the fighting music fans and lumber-jacket women, and the religious people yelling for quiet, and the excited people in the lineup at the bar who thought they were crashing a wedding. Suddenly the din was split by the loudest yell I have ever heard. Kelly screamed, "Shut up!" at the top of his lungs. He had gen- uinely loved Diana, and he just couldn't take the disre- spectful behavior anymore. Everyone stopped what they were doing and looked at Kelly. And then, unbelievably, everybody, even the stupidest and drunkest people, went quiet and started to listen to Elton John sing about "England's Rose." Somebody went and turned off "Give the Dog a Bone" on the truck stereo. The scream woke my dad, who was still sleeping outside in the car, and he wandered into the hall to listen. Everyone stopped and listened; the Elks guy stopped serving beer. It was quite a moment.

Dad put his hand on my shoulder. The crowd standing outside Westminster Abbey was completely undone, sob- bing openly. The crowd in Driftwood Hall sobbed too as the last strains of the song came from the TV. The religious people even hugged the drunken, weepy Kelly after it was all over and said, "God bless."

Garth Brooks replaced AC/DC on the stereo. "We already heard some. You go for it, man," were the touching words from the head banger to the country fan. Marcus's girlfriend finally went to sit on his knee. Before I knew it, everybody was dancing to Garth Brooks. Finn grabbed me and MacGregor and added us to the end of a line dance, which was just basically a conga line, because most of the people were too drunk to do more than kick their legs out to the side like they had a mouse up their pantleg and then stagger backward.

Can you believe it? I danced at Driftwood Hall! Life Experience Number 2010! The line dance fell apart when one of the lumber-jacket women tackled Finn and wrestled him away for some up-close-and-personal two-stepping. I guess she hadn't heard.

Weirdest of all, Jack snuck up to me in this very top-secret way and tapped me on the shoulder. When I turned around, he mumbled something I couldn't hear.

"What?"

He shuffled around in his high-tops and looked over his shoulder.

"Sorry about, you know, everything."

I was so floored, all I could do was stare. Then, shuffling even faster, like he was willing himself to disappear, he said, "Your hair's cool. Don't, ah–" He didn't get to finish because Kevin staggered toward him, leaning forward at an unsustainable angle.

"Man, I am so fried," he slurred, as Jack broke his fall, too drunk to even notice me.

"Shit," Kevin said, as Jack got him stabilized. I walked away, shaking my head in shock. Shit indeed.

So in the end, even though Dad let MacGregor drive home, saying it was his turn, I still feel that I can call myself a driver *and* a dancer. And even though I didn't really talk to anyone, and only danced with my dad and younger brother, I didn't get into any fistfights and people spoke to me, and that is definitely progress.

September 8

Just when I thought life would go disappointingly dull and I'd have nothing to look forward to ever again, I got incredible news! My family is leaving the Dark Ages and heading into the Enlightenment. Or at least the computer age. We are finally getting a computer. With a modem! We are only the last people in the civilized world to get one. Bob's very excited for me. He says being computer literate and comfortable on the Web is essential for anyone who wants to be a cultural critic. Maybe there's some sort of Cliff Notes version of *The Lord of the Rings* available online for those of us who are finding it hard to make the transition from *The Hobbit.*

I'd suspect that being a cultural critic, I will probably show a lot of natural ability in Web design. Or at least in Internet surfing. I haven't really shown any special talent in computer class at school, but I think that's just because real Web people work at night in the privacy of their own homes. Plus I take computers at the Alternative, and due to some of the students' lack of respect for authority and the female form, they've had to install a lot of security so the computers can only access a few sites now, like the Anglican Church directory.

We are getting the computer from some friend of my mother's who is tired of modern life and is selling her system so she can get a loom. The friend doesn't want to be able to work from home anymore. She probably doesn't want to work from anywhere, if she's like most of my parents' loser friends.

She's supposed to drop it off tonight. Dad thinks he will set it up, but I bet MacGregor will end up having to do it. Dad's excited because he's going to write his "bodice rippers" on the new computer instead of on his typewriter. He used to say that he was a traditionalist from the old school and that's why he didn't word-process, but I think it's because he (a) doesn't know how to use a computer, and (b) doesn't write enough to justify a hard drive.

Mom is excited about making flyers for the folk music society (I'm sure they will be marvels of design and typography), but she's nervous about electromagnetic fields. MacGregor is looking forward to doing research about bugs and fish. Myself, I just plan to soak up Internet culture, you know, how people talk to each other and stuff. Maybe I'll write a paper about the Internet. The paper will be so good that it will be clear that I am ideally suited to a career in Internetting. Who knows, the essay may even be groundbreaking for my age category. I wouldn't be surprised if it got me immediate job offers from, like, *Wired* magazine or something.

Later
Well, they've been at it for hours, and my father retreated long ago to the basement in frustration. It's always like this when anything mechanical has to be done around here. Dad thinks that because he used to be a musician, he is "quite handy." Personally, I don't think that the ability to plug an electric guitar into an amp translates into technical

wizardry. That particular delusion leads to disappointment for my father every time.

MacGregor and Mom are climbing all over the computer trying to get all the plugs and cables straightened out. So far they have managed to achieve a loud hum from the box part, but the TV part is still black. I hope the hum isn't signaling some kind of irreparable damage to the thing's innards. Mom and MacGregor are not being very gracious about the advice I have been kind enough to give them. From my vantage point on the couch, I think I am in a good position to call out directions and insights.

Mom yelled, "For the love of God, don't help!" a few times, but I ignored her ingratitude. They wouldn't have gotten nearly so far without my assistance. Except for my suggestion that they get a professional because they were never going to make it work, I have been quite encouraging.

Watching them work is boring, so I think I'll go have a nap and read some *Fellowship*. I certainly hope they have the thing working by the time I get up. I have a lot of Web discovery in front of me.

Late

So apparently the stupid thing is working. Everybody has been taking turns doing their activity on the computer, but they are all giving me the big freeze. Mom says it's because I was such a pain in the ass when it was being hooked up.

I have assured my incredibly selfish family that I don't

need their help, that I am perfectly capable of figuring it out myself. I am sitting here in my room until they go to bed. When they are asleep, I will surf the Net all night if I want. Screw them.

Still later

Well, so far Internet culture sucks. I'm not even sure if I am on the Web or not. If this is it, all these stupid little boxes on the screen, then the Internet is the biggest fraud I've come across yet. I think there is supposed to be some kind of noise when the computer hooks up to the Net, but so far all I've gotten is these clanking sounds and squawks and beeps when I hit the keys.

I can't take this anymore. I'm going to go wake up MacGregor.

Really late

It turns out I was in the Help menu. I don't know how a person is supposed to tell what's going on with these computers. Anyway, MacGregor showed me how to get online. You have to hit a bunch of commands and then the computer makes this whirring noise, and then you do a few more commands, and then you look for things by their names.

It all seems pretty time-consuming to me. I certainly don't feel like I'm entering a whole new realm of communication or anything. I'm going to look at some Web pages and try and find a chat room. MacGregor left me some *Idiot on the Internet* book to help. I would prefer a more serious manual, but it's all I've got. So far I don't see much in the way of career opportunities on the Internet, unless I want to be professionally frustrated for a living.

September 10
The number of perverted things on the Internet is mind-boggling. It didn't matter what I looked up last night, everything that came up was about sex. I looked up careers and got all these ads for Big Bouncy Bimbo Will Do the Job and Cyber Slut Goes to Work. Unbelievable. The Internet is a sewer.

The whole thing is disturbing. I mean, I have spent only a couple of hours on the Net and I am pretty much corrupted. I looked at some of those dirty Web pages, and the stuff on them is totally disgusting. I am only fifteen years old. I just shouldn't have access to some things. Things like my mother's and father's failure as human beings and explicit Internet perversions.

Also, it takes forever to see anything on the stupid Web. I don't think it's a good idea to waste my youth waiting for porn pages to download in the mistaken hope that they will contain something enriching or helpful. If it takes this long just to look at a web site, I can't even imagine how long it takes to make one.

I still haven't found a chat room. Given my lack of conversational skills, it's just as well.

Later

I guess web sites can tell when you visit them, or what-ever. I know because several of the sex sites I tried to look at last night sent us e-mails today. My dad got them when he checked our mail in this depressingly hopeful sort of way that I can already tell is going to get on my nerves.

The only e-mails we got were thanks-for-stopping-in-at-our-filthy-site type greetings, followed by advertise-ments for FREE LIVE GIRLS FREE LIVE GIRLS FREE LIVE GIRLS.

Dad, thinking he was being very witty, wrote them back and said:

yes, by all means free the live girls

He is already doing that no-capitals thing that you're supposed to do if you are an e-mail hipster. Anyway, Dad said he was disappointed in my choice of websites and hoped I had gotten it out of my system. Mom said the com-puter and the Internet were supposed to be for educational purposes and were not to be abused. Blah, blah.

They probably think I have some kind of sex problem now. If being disinterested to the point of asexuality is a problem, then I guess I've got one. Other than that, I'm fine. Except I am pretty exhausted from staying up all night surfing the lame-o Web.

Later

The Internet has become quite the family togetherness tool. This afternoon I found something called the Butt Page. It's a whole web site devoted to detailing the things misguided thrill seekers put up their rear ends that they later have to have removed at the hospital.

Is this any sort of education for a young girl? I think not.

Anyway, I stumbled on the page when I was looking up my favorite band, and one of the only two CDs I own, the Ass Ponys. I found the Butthole Surfers, and then the Butt Page instead of the Ass Ponys.

The Butt Page is done by some doctor at a hospital in what must be quite a big city, judging from just the sheer numbers of people who check in with this problem and the incredible varieties of items that become " anal lodgings."

After I discovered the page, I called MacGregor over to see an amazing X ray of a "misplaced" screwdriver. He said he'd heard of the site but thought it was just an urban legend. Dad came over to tell me to stop misusing the Internet, but as soon as he saw the list of objects, he pulled up a chair. Mom, an eavesdropper of the highest order, started to give us a lecture on human dignity and all that sort of crap, but she too was hooked the second she saw the case study of the lawyer who had been admitted three times to have an avocado removed from his nether regions and who still refused psychiatric help. I didn't think that we, as a family, were capable of degenerating much further. Apparently I was wrong.

September 14

Well, it looks like I'm not much better with friends in cyberspace than I am in person. I finally found a chat room and talked to a few people. It was an unsatisfactory experience all around.

Right away I was irritated by people's handles. There's something kind of pathetic about having to make up your own nickname in the first place. And then when you choose one like Big Kahuna or Lizard King or Sexy Stuff, well, that's just plain embarrassing.

The first chat room I got into was supposed to be about careers or livelihoods or something. I thought it was actually kind of virtuous of me to go to a room like that. I was hoping that it would impress my parents if they happened to walk by. So anyway, I got into this room and made a few comments. I don't know if I got the cutesy computer-geek punctuation wrong or what, but the chatters immediately started getting hostile.

There was some stupid conversation already going on when I got into the room.

Apollo commented:

is it not true that cultural and gender constructs are the products of specific historical and cultural transformations as well as the hegemony of the powerful elites?

Athena responded:

that may be true but it must also be remembered that such constructs must be viewed through the lens of a mediating nature, the reciprocity of marriage, the socialization of children, transforming raw foodstuffs into meals, and the multiple discourses of civilization.

I couldn't understand what they were talking about, so I tried to get the conversation going a bit. I typed in:

hi! hey what’s up with that butt page on the web, eh? does anyone want the address? you should really check it out. it’s really gross!! **^+

Apollo:
what??

Me:
isn’t this the careers in culture chat room? i wouldn’t mind discussing the ass ponys or maybe courtney love, since she’s pretty controversial and everything. i hear she goes on the web quite a bit. if we discuss her she might even visit! i’m interested in maybe doing cultural studies or something with computers for a living but i’m still in school right now.

Athena:
this is the comparative cultural studies room for the unified analysis working group at the university of western washington . . .

Apollo:
and we are trying to have a serious discussion.

I thought that was rude, especially after I was so nice and everything. I typed:

well, excuse me very much, but I’ve read a few things and i know that the web is open to anyone. it is the last truly democratic place on earth and i can be here if i want.&^”{/** if i want to talk about careers in popular culture you can’t stop me@$$&

Athena:
ok. we, the majority, vote that you get out so we can have our seminar in peace.

For all I knew there were lots of other people in the chat room who were bored into silence by Athena and Apollo's terrible conversation. To encourage them I tried to liven things up:

i think courtney love is a major talent, even though i wasn’t allowed to see the people vs. larry flynt. please respond all those hole fans! !! *.*^*

Apollo:
look. we're trying to have a meeting here. we don't care about hole or courtney love. we're academics.

Athena:
there's no one here but us.

Me:
i think that courtney and madonna would be evenly

matched in a fight because madonna works out at least five hours a day but she's no spring chicken anymore, and courtney’s tough and everything but rumor has it she’s weakened by drug addiction. ??:@^## and for all you lord of the rings fans, i’m on page 32 and really loving it!!!!!

Apollo:
for god's sake just ignore him.

Athena:
all right. well, as I was saying, the analytical domains are not dichotomous, but rather continua.

Apollo:
true, you posit a valid perception. it is often imputed that such dichotomous thinking is a uniquely western phenomenon.

Me:
the butt page can be found at _____

Nobody answered me, and Apollo and Athena kept having their stupid conversation. I gave up.

That's it for chat rooms. They're full of snobs and freaks, just like the rest of the world. The shabbiness of Internet culture just goes to show that people cannot be trusted. Give them a bit of free time and all of a sudden the world is filled with people documenting the items other people put up their bums and talking gibberish to each other 24/7. The least we can do is keep all that self-involvement and perversion private.

September 16
Well, the family fascination with the computer hasn't lasted. Too much like work for some people, I guess. MacGregor is the only one who still uses it. Dad has stopped, I think because he really doesn't function well upstairs. Mom couldn't handle the idea of the electromagnetic fields coming off the monitor. She was terrified that her ovaries were being affected. I haven't the heart to tell her that her ovaries are too old to matter. She's a bit long in the tooth for concerns about the health of her reproductive organs, if you ask me.

Bob thinks I'm making good progress on my cultural criticism. Today he brought in a tape of what he called the "most exciting, empowering show on TV." It's called *Buffy the Vampire Slayer*, and I have to admit, it was totally amazing. It seemed a little risky, enjoying something so . . . fun, but I couldn't help it. We watched two episodes, and by halfway through the second episode pretty much every Teen in Trouble was piled into Bob's office. Everybody loved it. Too bad Buffy wasn't on when I was in first grade. If I'd gone to school dressed like her instead of a hobbit, my life would have been very different.

September 17

Mom borrowed an old lead apron to shield us all from the electromagnetic fields coming off the computer. She got it from her hippie dental assistant friend who doesn't need it because she has trouble keeping a job. This friend likes to wear those sleeveless batik dresses, which wouldn't be so bad, but she's one of those uncontrolled-growth-of-body-hair types, and her armpits are a bit much for the clients. They lie there helpless while she drags her pit hair across their faces. The result is that she hardly ever needs her lead apron. She's lent it to Mom, who now uses it when she has to water the forest of plants that she has put all around the computer. You can hardly even see the computer anymore because there are so many plants around it. Apparently Mom has decided that the plants will absorb the toxins that are supposedly leaking from the screen. Somebody should tell her that our twenty-year-old TV is probably quite a bit more hazardous than the computer. The TV was made before there were any safety regulations about appliances, and it's probably doing us serious cellular damage every time we turn on *CBC News* or *Road to Avonlea*. I don't think it's even capable of hooking up to cable or a satellite or anything, which is what we'll need if I'm going to get access to *Buffy*.

Mom makes MacGregor wear the lead apron every time he uses the computer. How he manages to keep his dignity with a thirty-pound sheet of lead squishing him into the chair is beyond me. He can barely see over it. I enjoy watching her dash over to put the apron on him, contorting her body to shield her vulnerable ovaries, and then scurrying away into the kitchen to pore over her detoxification books.

MacGregor seems immune to all the perversions and distractions on the Net. He clicks away intently, once in a while printing out some bit of information about making your own food mix for your fish, or about the breeding cycles of the Lake Malawi cichlid or something. He calls for someone to get him out from under the apron when he's done.

He has been e-mailing some fish expert guy to get advice on his tanks. Apparently this e-mail guy is impressed with MacGregor's "commitment to the hobby" and his "good, solid fish-keeping skills." I know this because I've been reading their e-mails.

The expert suggested that MacGregor bring his fish to a fish show and auction down in Terrace. The idea is incredible, when you think about it. People drag their poor fish down to some community center, make them do their stuff (whatever stuff it is that fish do), and then sell them. You have to wonder who thought this idea up. Somebody with a lot of imagination, apparently.

At first it struck me as a little bizarre that MacGregor would be into a fish show. I mean, it seems exploitative or something. But then he explained to me that according to his expert, fish shows help to establish breeding standards and are very informative if you are planning to get into line breeding. Of course. Why hadn't I thought of that? Anyway, MacGregor's very excited about meeting his pen pal, who is supposedly pretty famous among fish types for his research and because he's bred a couple of kinds of fish that have never been bred in captivity before. I know I'm practically at a standstill with excitement.

Mom said she would drive MacGregor down to Terrace for the show in a couple of weeks, and they filled out the entry form and e-mailed it off to Mr. Fish Expert. A few of the angelfish babies and their cannibal parents (I guess they won't be strutting their parenting skills) and one of MacGregor's bettas (the Siamese fighting fish) will be going to the show. I've convinced my parents to let me go by playing the guilt card. They are very conscientious about not playing favorites. I don't have those hangups. I'm clear that MacGregor is my favorite.

I want to go to the show to see whether there will be any tricks performed by the fish or whether it will be straight swimming. I also want to go because my life is boring.

Mom told me that I am not to have one of my "episodes," whatever that's supposed to mean. Any episodes I have are a direct reaction to some unbearable behavior of hers. The sooner we get that straight, the better off we all will be.

MY VANCOUVER COUSIN

September 18

Big news. Bigger even than fish shows. My cousin Frank is going to come to school here! This is so cool. Apparently after she ran away from here, she finally turned up home in Vancouver and actually did part of her drug treatment, but she didn't need to finish because, according to Uncle Laird, she wasn't as sick as most of the people in the program who hadn't been given her advantages. Frank told Uncle Laird that what she really wanted was to go to school like a regular kid. Everyone is taking that as a really good sign. So Uncle Laird is working on getting her into some very exclusive private school for gifted geniuses in Vancouver. Frank isn't exactly a model student or anything, so he is going to have to pull some strings and call in some favors. In the meantime Frank is going to go to school with me. Now there will be two of us who don't fit in!

I wonder if Frank will notice and be impressed by my new fashion statement. I'm ready for more peer interaction. I mean, I know Life Goal No. 2 is supposed to be about increased contact with people outside of immediate family. But Frank isn't exactly family. She's a distant-enough relative that she could be a friend, especially now that I'm a bit cool and more worldly than I was. I could be ready to take the big step into a friendship. Frank would be the perfect peer group. She is even more different than me! I wonder if she watches *Buffy* and reads *The Lord of the Rings*.

September 21

Frank is here. Her look has completely changed again. She has gone completely boy, with huge overalls, a black toque, and man-sized silver platform sneakers.

Frank doesn't seem interested in talking. I guess in that way she hasn't changed. She went straight to her room when she got here and hasn't come out yet. That was this morning, and now it's almost dinnertime. Mom says that Frank has a lot of readjusting to do and that she is so talented and smart that it may take a while for the effects of her old lifestyle to wear off and for her to get used to normal family life again. I love the way my mom implies that Frank's specialness is related to the fact that she's a blood relative. Also, I think Mom has made a pretty big leap by assuming that our family in any way represents normal family life.

Mom has arranged for Frank to go and see Death Lord Bob. A couple of gripping sessions with the greatest mind in modern teen counseling should set her right for sure.

School tomorrow and I get to bring Frank! Excellent.

September 22

Frank did not disappoint today. My mom had to knock on her door for about half an hour this morning before she finally answered.

"Meet you downstairs," Frank yelled from behind the door.

They were the first words she had spoken since she arrived. MacGregor and I were waiting near the front door, and Mom was whispering worriedly with Dad at the kitchen table about what they would do if she wouldn't come out of her room, when Frank finally emerged. She appeared at the top of the stairs wearing the back-to-school outfit from hell.

Frank had on knee-high athletic socks with what looked and sounded like white patent leather tap shoes, one of those yellow poodle skirts like they used to wear in the fifties, a tiny pink T-shirt with DADDY'S LITTLE SWEET-HEART written on the front in glittery silver letters, and a blond wig with the ends flipped up. She sounded like a team of polo ponies coming down the stairs in her tap shoes.

We all stared as Frank reached the main floor, twirled, sending her skirt flying out around her, and held out her miniature stuffed-animal backpack and asked for some lunch.

Outstanding. Frank is going to be even more fun than I had hoped.

Later

Frank came with me to Math for Reluctant Adders at the Alternative school. At the start of class Doug the Concerned said, "Hey you guys, I want to introduce you to a new classmate. This is Frank, and she is joining us from Vancouver."

Everyone had been staring at us since we walked in, like maybe Frank was joining us from Mars. Frank looked directly at Doug with a smirky little smile on her lips. She turned her head and slowly, one by one, scanned everyone in the room. Then she flipped her wig hair around a few times, clicked her tap shoes against the floor, and stared out the window. She didn't say a word.

About fifteen or twenty minutes later Frank put up her hand.

"May I be excused to use the washroom?" she asked.

Doug very jovially gave her permission, informing her, "We don't stand on ceremony around here. Do what you need to do. Just make sure you come back, eh? Ha ha."

She grabbed her knapsack and out of the room she clicked. And didn't come back.

I caught a glimpse of her at lunch. She was in the middle of a bunch of jocks with square heads. I didn't get a very good look, but she seemed to be doing some sort of a tap routine. The boys stood in a circle around her, looking dumbfounded.

Frank didn't get home until after midnight. Mom and Dad were huddled downstairs in their matching ratty bathrobes, probably discussing how to break it to Uncle Laird that they had lost Frank again, when what sounded like a muscle car without a muffler pulled up. I lost no time getting downstairs so I wouldn't miss any of the action.

We could hear male laughter and shouting as the car sputtered, growled, and belched. Then the sound of doors opening and slamming and opening and slamming. More laughter. Then what sounded like someone getting sick and somebody else screaming out obscenities. A chorus of chugging noises and cans being crumpled. Then in walked Frank.

She looked pretty much the same as she did when she left in the morning, but she was wearing a fluorescent orange Canadian National Rail vest over her T-shirt and her wig was on crooked. The bangs lurched into one eye and the flip was askew.

Frank clattered into the house, weaving slightly starboard, and asked brightly if she had missed dinner. Outside, the car was revving its engine and somebody with a disturbingly old voice shouted, "I love you, baby!" Then tires squealed as the car screeched away. Frank didn't seem to hear. She blinked at Mom and Dad, wished us good night, and made her way unsteadily up the stairs to her room. My mother and father looked shell-shocked. I probably should've prepared them for this sort of thing a bit by going out sometimes. Poor things.

I've borrowed all of Bob's episodes of *Buffy* and left them around so Frank can see that I am into cool cult-type TV shows. Maybe she'll want to watch a few episodes with me.

September 23
Another outstanding Frank day.

Mom took a more aggressive approach to getting Frank out of bed this morning. When Frank didn't answer the first knock, Mom marched right into her room, totally crashing Frank's personal boundaries in the process. It was a big step for Mom, because she takes the whole personal space thing very seriously. I think that waking Frank up was supposed to be some kind of harsh punishment designed to put her on the straight and narrow. I have my doubts about how effective it will be.

Frank didn't wake up even with Mom standing at her head calling her name, so Mom physically lifted her out of bed. It was really excellent to watch. Mom tried to get her to sit up, but Frank was like a floppy rag doll. Dad made me come away and stop watching. He said it was none of my business and that I should "stop being such a little voyeur." That from the King of the Voyeurs!

Finally Mom came downstairs, alone, red-faced, and winded, with her hair mussed up.

"Frank will be down shortly and then we are leaving!" she announced in a voice that suggested she was ready to take on anyone who dared argue with her. Another bonus of having Frank come to school is that now we get a ride to school, I think because my parents are worried she won't get there on her own.

Then Mom turned to my dad.

"I suppose it would have killed you to help me with her?"

Dad put down his coffee cup and informed her that this whole thing—meaning, I suppose, Frank staying with us—was not his bright idea.

Mom went off about how she needed his support in the affairs of the household and he said that the household had about twice as many affairs since Frank moved in, and they argued back and forth until Frank finally came down-stairs.

She was wearing her monster overalls with the silver sneakers and a BMX shirt, and for some reason she had a racing number tied to her back. The crotch of her overalls hung down almost to her knees, and when she moved, it looked like she had short mutant legs. Unless you saw her from the side, in which case the giant overalls dipped so low at her hips, you could see her striped boy underwear and a good portion of her bare legs.

Frank also had on huge mirrored sunglasses and the black toque pulled low. She seemed shrunken since yes-terday and got even smaller when Dad asked her loudly how her hangover was. Mom bustled around trying to act like she was in control of her life and yelled, needlessly I thought, for us all to get in the car. It was awesome to feel like the golden child for once. This must be how MacGregor feels all the time.

We all piled into the antiglamor wagon and off we went. Frank pulled a huge pair of headphones out of her knapsack and sat huddled in the corner of the backseat and bobbed her head weakly. I hope she stays with us forever. She seems so frail.

Later

Frank lasted almost all the way through Ms. Swinke's class on Positive Life Choices. She might not have made it that far, but she fell asleep almost as soon as she sat down. Ms. Swinke, who was just coming off a week on stress leave, was upset—"Excuse me? Excuse me!"—and to me—"What is wrong with your cousin?" I told her that Frank suffered from narcolepsy. Ms. Swinke immediately got all proactively supportive and positive and was glad that we had some mentally ill, special needs, handicapped-type participation in the class. In my opinion we're a little overrepresented in that department already, but I'm not complaining. Swinke gave a fist-pumping talk on equal access to education and the rights of the differently abled. That was okay, since she stopped talking about positive life choices for a while, which is possibly the worst subject in the world.

When Frank finally woke up, stretched, and asked if she could be excused to use the washroom, Ms. Swinke fell all over herself giving directions to the handicapped washroom and urging Frank to pass on any comments she had about the school's facilities to her, Ms. Swinke, who would be honored and empowered to give them to the proper authorities. Frank scratched her head under her toque and said, "Yeah, thanks," and left. She didn't come back.

September 24
Frank didn't come home at all last night. Mom got completely unhinged and Dad suggested that perhaps all her New Age philosophies hadn't prepared her for the reality that life isn't all love and miracles; sometimes it is just screwed-up teenagers who are completely selfish and out of control and best left for professionals to deal with. Then they had a huge argument and Dad went to sleep in the basement.

They still weren't speaking this morning, but by dinnertime they seemed to have worked things out. My mother told MacGregor and me at dinner that even though she wanted to help Frank experience a normal life, she and Dad were not going to allow Frank to tear our family apart.

The truce lasted until Mom realized that Frank probably wasn't coming home tonight either. Then she and Dad had a fight about whether they should call the police or go out looking for Frank themselves. Dad thought they should watch TV and go to bed and said that Frank had more street smarts than the rest of the town combined, and that instead of rescuing Frank maybe they should post warnings for the innocent townsfolk that she was on the loose. Mom was not amused.

She was even less amused when this fortyish biker type with a droopy mustache, still-wet slicked-back hair, and a leather vest arrived at the door with flowers and asked for Frank. It was great to watch Mom try to be polite yet cool and maintain her New Age delusion that bad things can't happen to good families, even with seedy semi-outlaws showing up on the doorstep to court her runaway teenage niece.

Today at my session all Bob wanted to talk about was Frank and "how we were going to help her." It was a relief since Frank is more interesting to talk about than me. It was particularly a relief since I got a big intervention at school today in the counseling boiler room.

Doug the Concerned took me aside after Life Skills class (How to Get Out of Bed and Have Breakfast and Why

You Should 101) to ask how I was. He said I seemed distracted, but not in my usual way. Apparently he is worried that I feel displaced by all the attention paid to Frank. Man, I can't believe him. We are each allotted a certain amount of child-in-crisis time at the Alternative. Because I am fairly new, I was getting quite a bit more child-in-crisis time than most of the other people in my school. Plus it's probably more interesting for Mr. Richards and the other professional carers to use their psychological techniques to try to get me to talk about my problems than to have to listen to Violet the Victim tell one of her well-known ghastly tales again. Frank better come back. She makes life worth living.

September 26
Frank came back today. Well, she didn't actually come back on her own. My mom had to go and get her from the back office at Zellers, where she was being held for shoplifting. I thought she had better taste, and I said so to Mom, who, defensive as always, informed me that Frank had been into the watches, which were actually quite nice. Apparently Frank was wearing stuff from all over town under her monster overalls. She was so layered up with stolen goods that she had trouble running when the security guy went after her, which is how she got caught.

Mom somehow convinced the store not to press charges, and the police told her that she had better keep her niece under control. I think it may even have been Officer Ross from the parking lot fight who let Frank go.

He must have a bit of a soft spot for my mom and her teenagers. As a family, we are probably getting a terrible reputation with the authorities, which is sort of funny when you think about it, considering how hard Mom tries to keep our happy hippie family image together. I personally think it's kind of cool that we're known by name to law enforcement officials.

Mom took Frank straight from Zellers to an appointment with Death Lord. I wonder how many Franks Bob has come across in his extensive counseling experience. Hah! I wonder if Bob's going to do a Mrs. F. under the strain. It took me four years to get Mrs. F. to the breaking point. Frank'll probably crack Bob in just a couple of days!

Anyway, Frank is in her room now and has said she's going to clean up her act. Mom is convinced that the session with Death Lord has turned things around. I have my doubts. Frank is actually going to stay home tonight. I asked her why, and she said something about Friday being amateur night and then went upstairs to go to bed. It was four o'clock. Frank certainly is old for her age.

Later

Mom and Dad informed me and MacGregor at dinner tonight that we are going to take Frank on the Annual Family Trail Ride with the Northern Saddle Sores tomorrow. Mom used to have horses when she was young, and for some reason she is convinced that trail riding is this tremendously bonding and healing activity for us as a family. The Saddle Sores trail rides are the only community-type events that our family does. Horse people are pretty wild, and these rides always degenerate into serious debauchery. How Mom could think that these events are healthy is beyond me. I doubt Frank has ever been on a horse. But who knows? The trail ride might be my chance to really get to know Frank. We could use the time to get our friendship going. So far we haven't really talked much. I don't know if she's noticed all the changes in me yet. It's time I showed her. I am ready to let peer pressure take its toll! I am willing to be influenced! I am going to accomplish Life Goal No. 2: Increase contact with people outside of immediate family.

Another suitor arrived with flowers for Frank a minute ago. I think he's the clerk from the jewelry counter at Zellers. Mom yelled at him and Dad laughed.

September 28
Where to start?

We got up at about six A.M. to get ready for the ride. Dad wore the same incredibly embarrassing getup he wears on the ride every year: jeans, an ultrasuede jacket with fringe, and a cotton fishing hat. The Mensa geniuses all wear the same thing except Finn, who wears his usual uniform of pilled-on-the-ass dress pants and satin bomber jacket with the idiotic cotton fishing hat. Oh yeah, but instead of crappy loafers he wears crappy vinyl ankle boots. It took Mom forever to wake up Frank. While we waited for her to get dressed, we had to listen to Mom get frustrated trying to fit all the health food and booze into the packs.

I'm not sure what kind of ride Frank thought we were going on, but I'm guessing it wasn't a community horseback ride. She came downstairs wearing a shiny red one-piece jumpsuit covered with blue and yellow stars, black-and-white-striped leg warmers, some kind of half-bald feather boa, and silver slippers.

Dad and MacGregor stood staring at her with their mouths open. Mom, who was obviously jealous, told Frank that she looked wonderful but that slippers were inappropriate for riding. Mom made her put on a pair of old cowboy boots, which made her look like a confused cowgirl superhero.

And off we went to Tex's place. He lives on a ranch out near Driftwood Hall. His spread has very nice fences, which is apparently an indication of how successful his big game guide-outfitter business is. He is a kingpin in the Smithers Saddle Sores club and lends horses to anyone who shows up for the annual ride without one. Well, actually he lends them pack ponies, which are sort of a lesser form of horse, as far as I can tell. For most of the attendees from town, the ride is the only time they get on a horse all year. And the only reason they get on the horse is to get loaded in a slightly different setting.

Dad and the other Mensa members worship Tex to an unhealthy degree. They all wish they were him, and their riding outfits are part of a sad effort to look like him. Tex has a lot of facial hair and dresses like a mountain man. He speaks only to make manly-type comments, and around him all the other men seem like frail grade-school girls. I don't think he even has any electricity in his house.

Tex is notable because he is so armed. You would think he was American. His third wife shot him when he left her for another woman, and even after all that he still keeps a rifle rack in every room in his house and one in the barn. According to my dad, "Now that's guts." Tex is at least sixty-five or even older and on his fifth wife, who is around twenty-four years old. Mom doesn't disapprove of Tex like she does of Marcus, because it's understood that Tex's wives work so hard, they have to be young. Tex's latest wife, Gloria, is so strong she is almost as manly as Tex.

Tex's hunting clients are usually American business-men who fly into town wearing full combat gear and car-rying semiautomatic machine guns in gun warmer sleeves. They pay Tex huge amounts of money for a big game hunt. I think they would probably pay just to hang out with Tex for a while. Probably the whole guided hunt is just an inconvenience they go through to spend time with the pure manliness and testosterone that is Tex.

When we got to Tex's place, all the people without horses were being outfitted by Tex's wife and his guides, Bone and Eugene. They are the original something-to-prove brothers. Even though they aren't all that short, they spend a lot of energy overcompensating for not being tall. They stay on their horses as much as possible, and the rest of the time totter around on high-heeled boots. Their giant white cowboy hats add a good ten inches to their height, and they're so skinny, they look like matching hat and boot racks. Bone and Eugene are from Houston, which is about an hour from Smithers and even smaller, but they're sure never to correct out-of-towners who think they're from Houston, Texas.

Today their younger sister, Georgette, was with them. She goes to school in Houston, but I'd seen her around town a few times. She didn't look happy to be on the trail ride. She sat on her horse over by herself, looking cranky.

Marcus and Kelly were in Marcus's taxicab having a fight. Tex oversaw things with a kingly air.

Everyone connected with The Outfit, as Tex's place is called—Tex, Gloria, Eugene, and Bone—is cool in this very particular way: They all like to make dry little comments that make you feel like a waste of space. The Saddle Sores riders eat it up, just like Tex's more-money-than-brains clients. I personally think that enjoying being treated like a moron is a sign of poor self-esteem.

Tex strolled over as we pulled up. He looked at us, then squinted his eyes at Frank and said, "Them pants're gonna heat up somethin' fierce if yer plannin' on ridin' all day." Frank couldn't stay still long enough to listen to his remark, and by the time he finished, she was halfway across the yard. Dad, the shameless Tex worshiper, got all embarrassed and apologized for Frank's rudeness, but Tex just grinned and said, "Hell, I figure hot pants might be the point."

We all watched, mesmerized, as Frank gamboled over to meet Death Lord, who was pulling up in his decrepit, primer-covered El Camino. Tex had to poke Eugene and

Bone to get them to stop staring and keep working. I was sort of surprised to see Bob. He must really be settling into life in Smithers if he's showing up for this event.

It was madness for a while as people milled around with their borrowed packhorses and others arrived aboard their own horses or pulling their horse trailers behind their pickups.

Tex's steed was a huge palomino called Thunder or some other magnificent horse name like that. My pack pony was an unmagnificent little mare called Petunia. Marcus and Kelly got out of the cab and continued their argument aboard a pair of tiny bay ponies who had clearly seen better days. My father's was a tall, elderly horse in shades of dirty gray with a sagging lower lip.

Finally, after everyone was mounted, and Tex and Gloria handed out maps of the trail, Finn pulled up in his car with the Second Sport logo taped to the back windows. Finn is always late for everything. Tex rode over to make sure that Bone got Finn set up.

"Howdy," Tex growled. "Bone here'll look after you. Have a good ride."

Finn asked Bone if he could get one with "just a tad less dandruff, you know, for my allergies."

When Bone brought her over, it became obvious that Finn's horse was the absolute bottom of the barrel. She was a knock-kneed, swaybacked old brood mare with an attitude problem. When Finn clucked at her and slapped his legs against her sides, the horse laid her ears flat and snaked her head back to try to take a bite out of his leg.

Finn has been on the ride every year since I can remember, but he still doesn't seem to be clear on the mechanics of the bridle and reins. He just tried to get out of her way without falling off. He did a bit of a leapfrog maneuver behind the saddle and onto her rear. The old mare took the opportunity to do a bit of geriatric crowhopping. It was totally excellent to watch. Her stiff-legged bucks weren't exactly bronco material, but they made Finn yell. Dad and the other geniuses rushed over to try to get the mare calmed down and Finn straightened out.

"It won't stay still! It won't stay still. For God's sake, can't you keep it steady?"

By the time I finished watching Finn learn to ride again, Frank was long gone. I rushed to catch up.

Once on the trail, Dad, Marcus, Kelly, and Finn all rode together to share the "fortified" coffee. Mom set out to find some of her folk festival friends. I kept Petunia moving back and forth up and down the line of riders. First I tried to catch up to where Death Lord and Frank were riding, near the front of the line. I finally found Frank in the middle of a group of men including Eugene and Bone. She was pretending to lasso each of them in turn with her feather boa and making a big production of tossing her head back and laughing. Frank is very theatrical. I rode with them for a while, hoping maybe to start up a conversation, but no one really noticed me.

I rode Petunia so slowly that eventually the last-place geniuses caught up. By this time it was getting close to lunch, and they were thoroughly lubricated. Marcus and

Kelly continued the fight that had apparently begun when they went to pick up Marcus's girlfriend. They were fighting about whether Marcus should break up with her, because when they got to her house, she informed them that she was going to the Monster Truck Show in Houston with some other guy instead of the trail ride with Marcus. Marcus thought he should break up with her. Sensitive Kelly maintained that the Monster Truck girlfriend was "a really sweet girl" and she and Marcus had "something really special."

Dad was trying to draw out the story of the whole relationship from sordid start to pathetic finish. Not to be negative or anything, but they were not an impressive group in their ultrasuede jackets and cotton fishing hats, dissecting every little bit of meaning from the words and actions of some dim-witted nineteen-year-old floozy. I noticed Georgette riding close by, listening with fascination. After a few minutes I sped up Petunia and headed for the lunch area on Tex's map.

As I moved up the trail, Eugene rode up behind me. We were between groups on the trail, and he was the only other rider I could see. When I turned around to look at him, he smiled and asked how I was doing. I guess he was trying to start a conversation or something, but I wasn't really interested. I was focused on finding Frank so I could get our maturity-inducing friendship off the ground. And besides, Eugene's boots and hat suggested some pretty deep-rooted issues. He kept pace when I sped up again and didn't seem put off when I glared at him.

"Do you mind? I'm riding here," I said in my rudest voice.

"Nawdadawl," he said, making it into one long Texan-sounding word. I couldn't believe it. Next he would be trying to call me darling.

"So darlin'," he said, reaching over and pretending to adjust my saddle blanket a little too close to my leg, "you like ridin'?"

Before I could decide on a violent response, he was interrupted.

"Oh my God, Eugene! You are such a hormone in a hat!"

Georgette rode up right behind us.

Eugene turned bright red and pulled his huge white hat down over his eyes and took off.

"Sorry about my brother," she said. "Too many Nashville Network country music videos—that's where he gets all his brilliant pickup ideas. In fact, that's where he gets all his ideas."

"Uh, thanks."

"Yeah, no problem. You're Alice, right?"

"Yeah."

"I'm Georgette, reluctant sister of the rhinestone cowboy over there. I've seen you in the bookstore a few times."

"I don't work there anymore."

"Little too crunchy granola for you?" she asked.

"Something like that," I said.

"I like your shorts," she continued.

I almost thought I didn't hear her right. I mean, people usually aren't exactly falling all over themselves to compliment my fashion statement. Especially not people my own age.

"You mean my gauchos?"

"Is that what they're called?"

"Yeah. I got them in Prince George."

She looked impressed.

Georgette was dressed like a prethrifting me—plaid shirt and jeans.

She caught me looking.

"Ah, you know. I can't be bothered getting dressed up. I mean, I live in Houston, right? The idea is to get through and get out, you know what I mean?"

And I did, I really did.

"Well, I've got to get going. I have to find my cousin Frank. She's the one in stars."

Georgette laughed. "She's hard to miss."

She waved and I waved back and off we went.

By lunch the Saddle Sores Trail Ride was in full swing. Almost everyone had been drinking since we left the Outfit, and no one except the kids seemed interested in eating lunch.

Like I said, horse people are pretty wild. It seems like the minute even the most upstanding-type citizen gets a horse, some kind of cowboy-Lone Ranger thing comes over them and they start drinking heavily and having affairs and wearing "you can tell by my hat that I am a cowboy" clothes.

The lunch area on our ride up the Three Trails Pass

was a grassy field on a steep hillside. There were several weathered huts in various stages of decay in the clearing. The steady horses were left to wander free, grazing near their owners. The less reliable steeds were haltered and tethered to trees at the edge of the field. Knots of riders sat scattered around the field.

After a quick sprout sandwich I made my way over to where Frank sat in the middle of a group of men. She was singing old-fashioned cowboy songs complete with coyote noises and everything. Between songs she would lean over and chuck one of her audience under the chin. She was paying special attention to Bone, giving him extra chucks under the chin and lobbing her ratty old feather boa at him more than anyone else. Eugene looked jealously on, and Bob glanced worriedly back and forth between the two of them, holding tight to his sparse beard.

Over on the other side of the field, Tex was in the middle of a story about the time he rode his horse right into a bar in Hyder, Alaska, to escape a grizzly that had been following him. Tex's audience was almost as interested as Frank's.

I wandered from group to group watching people's inhibitions fall. They began to forget there were children present. MacGregor lay with his head on my mom's lap, reading a science book. Mom's friends got more and more specific about their sex lives. Mom, who'd had a few, didn't add much to the conversation but made no effort to shield MacGregor. She probably took comfort in the knowledge that when MacGregor reads, he doesn't hear anything, not even direct questions.

"Well, you would know, Diane. Come on, you sell the book at the store. You know, the one about tantric sex."

"No, really. I haven't read it."

"Well, it's out of this world. I swear. I practically levitated."

Laughter, squeals, giggles.

Dad and the rest of the geniuses had gathered around Tex, who was telling about the time he rode through inner-city Detroit on his horse on his way across North America. He met up with a bunch of crack dealers in the inner city and apparently they discussed survival in the street and survival in the bush, and it turns out that it's the same thing in both places.

Georgette sat listening and I thought about going to sit with her, but then I figured I'd better not push my luck. Our earlier conversation was one of the longest I'd had with a girl my age in years without the word *bitch* leaving someone's mouth. No, I couldn't take the risk.

I went looking for Frank but couldn't find her. Her horse was still tethered on the edge of the field, but she was nowhere to be seen. I asked Bob if he'd seen her, and in a strangled whisper he said that no, he couldn't find her either.

By this time it was late afternoon, and marital vows were beginning to break around the field. A few horse ladies were seen disappearing into the woods or the shacks with small, bowlegged men who were not their husbands.

Eugene came up and asked me if I had taken a look inside the far shed yet. I said I hadn't. He asked if I'd like to go see it. I told him to get away from me, but not in a mean voice. Then I asked if he'd seen my cousin Frank, and he broke into a coughing fit and turned away, saying he had to go check the horses.

Someone lit a fire in the middle of the field as the afternoon cooled and the hot dogs came out of the packs and barbecue sticks were sharpened.

It began to get dark.

Shortly afterward Mom found me and asked if I had seen Frank. I hadn't. Bob's frantic pacing around the field didn't seem to be producing any results. Mom thrust a package of tofu dogs into my hand, told me to go and eat with MacGregor, and announced that she was going to organize a search party.

Before she could get her plan off the ground, Tex came over and suggested that sending a bunch of inebriates into the pitch-black bush was maybe not the best idea. Then Mom started run-walking around the perimeter of the field calling Frank's name. Some of her folkie friends tried to help but got confused.

"Yoo-hoo! Oh Frank!"

"What? I thought her niece was lost. Who's Frank?"

"Maybe he's that counselor over at the club for screwed-up kids."

"Oh yeah? But wouldn't that make him her nephew?"

"I guess."

"I heard he's a cutie."

"Really?"

Peals of laughter and giggles.

"Yoo-hoo! Oh Frank! Cutie Pie! Come out, come out, wherever you are!"

Mom was interrupted in her jog around the field by a rock-faced horse lady who took Mom's arm and whispered something to her and pointed to one of the shacks, outside which Bob was now pacing. Mom's shoulders sagged for a second before she threw them back and hustled over to get Dad.

After a quick conversation Dad straightened his fishing hat and headed off to the shack. When Bob saw Dad coming, he turned on his heel and headed the other way. Then, obviously torn, he turned back to Dad. After a couple of directional struggles with himself, Bob finally met Dad at the door of the shack. They exchanged a few words, and Bob stood, looking shattered, when Dad turned impatiently away from him.

I would've gone in with Dad, but I noticed MacGregor watching everything. He looked small and tired, standing there holding his science book and rubbing his eyes. I went over and sat down with him. A few minutes later Frank emerged from the doorway with an embarrassed-looking Dad right behind her. Many minutes later Bone poked his head out and then slunk over to his horse. Only it wasn't there. It was being held by my mother, who slowly led it over to where he stood.

Bob decided this might be a good time to practice his

crisis-intervention skills and went to stand between my mother and Bone. It was a bad move, because Mom turned on him. I watched Bob get smaller and smaller and my mother get louder and louder. Bone stood absolutely still behind Bob, in an effort to escape notice. I heard the words *disbarment* and *malpractice* and "why the hell didn't you do something?" as my mom shouted at Bob that she wouldn't have believed that a counselor could be more incompetent than Mrs. Freison but now she'd seen it all. Bob protested feebly. "I tried. I'm so sorry. I couldn't–" Mom wouldn't listen.

Eugene, watching in the crowd, seemed to look relieved, but it could just have been my imagination.

I decided MacGregor had probably seen enough, so I took him to go and find our horses. Georgette came over and stood with us. She asked MacGregor questions about his book. She pretended not to hear my mother yelling at my counselor. And we pretended not to see her brother hiding behind Bob.

The rest of the trail riders lingered over the cleanup so they could hear what was going on. Georgette snarled, "Mind your own business," under her breath when a couple nearby started commenting on the situation in stage whispers so loud we could hear every word.

Finally Dad went over and put his arm around Mom and led her back to where MacGregor and Georgette and I stood waiting with our horses. He retrieved Frank, and we headed back down the trail.

"Coming?" I asked Georgette.

"No. I'd better wait for my brothers. God only knows what trouble they'll get into on the way down."

"Oh. Okay. Well, see you, Georgette."

"George," she corrected. "See you, Alice."

We rode back down the trail in silence, except for the odd murmur between Mom and Dad. I looked back at one point, and they were holding hands.

Frank didn't say a word to me, and I was too embarrassed to ask her any questions, even though I wanted to hear what happened. I wondered if she would have been impressed if she knew I had been invited to a shed too.

September 29

Frank didn't go to school today. Apparently the blisters on her rear made it too painful for her to move. She tried to get Mom to take her to the hospital this morning, but Mom said that if blisters were all she got from those hot pants, she should consider herself lucky. I personally think that was a bit shaming, but whatever. Frank was on the phone talking to Uncle Laird when I got home. She was checking to see when she could get into that private school. I heard her say, "You know, Daddy, Smithers doesn't have a lot to offer culturally."

She's definitely got a point there.

Mom and Dad told me tonight that there will be no more sessions with Death Lord Bob. They are writing a formal complaint to his supervisors. The letter says that Bob does not have "sufficient good judgment or decision-making skills to work with young people." Apparently Bob has called three times to apologize, but my mother won't take his calls. It doesn't seem fair to expect a junior counselor to handle someone like Frank. Poor Death Lord. I'm going to miss helping him. Plus the video sessions were quite fun.

September 30
So much for blood is thicker than water. I can't believe it. Frank ran away with Linda today!

I came home from school to find Linda standing in my hallway. I nearly had heart failure. I stopped dead in my tracks, and she looked at me with those dead blue eyes and said, "I'm waiting for Frank."

"Oh," I said.

And then I went upstairs to my room. On my way past Frank's room I looked in and saw her stuffing things into her stuffed-animal backpack. I watched as she ate a handful of pills that she took from a silver suitcase filled with bottles and baggies. Frank was a walking pharma-ceutical company.

"See ya later, kid," she said.

"Yeah. Okay," I replied.

I asked her where she was going, but she just straight-ened her wig and winked as she brushed past me. Watching from the second-floor window, I saw her and Linda get into a blue Firefly that I know for a fact belongs to the neighbors.

So much for my peer group-friend ambitions.

I went to bed.

October 1
I didn't feel well today, so I didn't get out of bed. I could hear the crisis about Frank and the stolen car going on downstairs—the neighbor's phone calls, Uncle Laird's phone calls, calls and a visit from Officer Ross (now practically an old family friend), fights and arguments between my mom and dad. It went on all last night and this morning. Usually I love that stuff. Not today, though. I must be coming down with something.

October 2
Today my parents tried to talk to me about the not-getting-out-of-bed thing. They think I'm depressed because of Frank. They think I have some unhealthy role model adoption-negative hero worship issues going on. Obviously that's not it. I just don't feel well. And the ceiling really is pretty interesting if you look at it long enough.

October 3
Not only am I back in therapy with Death Lord, but now he's doing home visits. Mom came into my room this afternoon to say I had a visitor. In walked Bob right behind her. His hair was all tortured looking, like he had been pulling it out at the roots, and he had big bags under his eyes.

He started right in. He should have handled things differently; he didn't want to betray anyone's trust; he's been punished (his practicum has been extended by six months), and the worst punishment is the guilt he feels; if I stay in bed my depression will just get worse; he knows I looked up to Frank; drugs can make very good, very attractive people do bad things; blah, blah, blah.

I finally got up just so Death Lord would leave. Apparently I will have to stay up now or he will come back.

I really don't know what he would do without me. I give him reason to live.

October 4

Things have calmed down around here since Frank ran away and I got out of bed. All I have to look forward to now is that stupid fish show.

And that sounds worse all the time too. Now Geraldine the Awful of the James Woods lookalike fame is going to come to the fish show with us. That's just what we need. We will go off to Terrace trailing plumes of musk and pot and B.O. Just the smell of her probably will be enough to kill the fish. It's almost enough to make me not go. The only small mercy is that Geraldine is leaving Jane the Car Girl at home. I guess Jane was invited but Mom said she couldn't smoke in our car, so she declined. I'm sure she'll be waiting in their car when Geraldine gets home. Their relationship is enough to make me question having children. In fact, I've been thinking about reproductive issues a lot since the trail ride and Frank's inspiring example. I've been reassessing Life Goal No. 4: Some sort of boy-girl interaction? I think I may need more

extensive interaction to truly accomplish this, so I have
uncrossed it and put it back on my list. Aubrey doesn't
really count, because most of our interaction consisted of
me avoiding him.

A more thorough attack on the problem is in order.
The accomplishment of Life Goal No. 4 may require sex.
And not just because of what I saw on the Internet. I
need a clear success. So far my achieved Life Goals err on
the side of incompleteness. And the ones that I have
completed seem boring. Like going back to school. I
thought that would be exciting for longer than just one
day. But already school in an institutional setting is almost
as boring as school in a dysfunctional home setting. Violet
the Victim is the only person who really talks to me. And
all she does is ask my opinion of her latest still life with
fruit.

I *will* be a success in my own life! I won't play some bit
role. I want to be the star of my own production! For a
more extensive boy-girl interaction, all I have to do is get
one other person to do what I want for a few minutes.
That shouldn't be impossible.

Later

Now not only is Geraldine the Awful coming with us, but
so is Pit Hair the Dental Assistant. They are going to a
drumming class planned for the same place and time as the
fish show. The worst part is that they wouldn't have been
able to go if we weren't going already.

If Mom packs any more hippie freaks into the car,

there won't be any room for me and MacGregor, never mind the fish. I know MacGregor agrees with me that Pit and Geraldine shouldn't come, but he is too polite to say anything.

I really don't know if I can stomach several hours in the same car with those women. Mom should get more working-class friends. All of Mom's friends, who are waitresses at Smitty's or clerks at Zellers or wherever, are actually potters or weavers or something artistic like that. It's all crap. I admire store clerks who don't think they are too good or brilliant or creative to be clerks. I admire the people who don't want to be something they are not. Give me someone who is good at helping that logger find just the right plaid shirt and who isn't always coming up with excuses for why they don't have a more fulfilling job, someone who lives for the weekend and admits it.

I talked to George about it today when she called. I wasn't actually going to mention that she phoned. I mean, it's not that big a deal. It only means the end of aloneness and the accomplishment of Life Goal No. 2 and everything.

I told her about Frank and the fish show. She told me about her brothers and Houston. I was on the phone *actually talking* for almost an hour! Nothing to get excited about, although my parents did. I could tell by the way they hovered around in the distance and kept walking past looking all nervous and happy when they realized I was talking to a peer-type person. Poor things.

It was really sort of pathetic. Anyway, I suppose I should adjust my Life Goals list, but I can't. It's too soon. Frankly I'm afraid to jinx my peer-friendship accomplishments through overconfidence. I told George that when I have my career as an unskilled worker, I vow to give the other sandwich shop employees the respect they deserve by not going on about all my ambitions. When I pass my GED at age forty, I won't sound off about it and make all my coworkers feel inadequate by comparison. George agreed with my approach. She said that she'd read and loved *The Hobbit* but that she hadn't yet made it through *The Lord of the Rings*. She's interested in watching *Buffy* with me sometime. The conversation we had was so good, I think it will give me the strength to get through the trip to Terrace, which is almost as small and even less cultural than Smithers. It doesn't have the Bavaria-theme Main Street with the cobblestone motif or the statue of a guy blowing a giant alpenhorn.

The whole drive will be taken up with talk of how broke Geraldine and Pit are and how they should get some sort of government allowance just for not using too much water for bathing or something. There is no way I am sitting next to either of them. Thank God our car is so huge. Pit and Geraldine should be able to fit in the front seat with Mom. It's the least they can do; after all, I invited myself along first.

GOOSEBOY AND THE GOOD HAIR DAY

October 5

I got my way. All the hippie babes are in the front seat together and MacGregor and I are in the backseat of the Wonderwagon. I had my Walkman on at full volume when we picked up Geraldine and Pit, so I don't know how Mom explained why we were in the backseat with the doors locked. Maybe she told them my attitude was contagious or something. I think that my negative energy disturbs them to the point that they're happy to stay as far away from me as possible.

My new headphones are just like Frank's—perfect for ignoring people. They are huge and they look like noise protectors on a hard hat. And even though they plug into my Walkman, they have an antenna on the side which I think is pretty cool and hiphop. Dad says they make me look like a sullen Martian. Whatever. As long as they drown out the tuneless sounds of hippie whining, I'm happy. I just wish they came with matching nose plugs.

Geraldine and Pit are in fine form. They are all excited about the "serendipity" and "synchronicity" of the drumming workshop being held in the same community center as the fish show. They've hand-painted stars and moons and goddesses and other stuff all over their big rawhide drums, which they're holding on their laps to get a "connection going." Oh man. Geraldine has mentioned a few times how sorry she is that Jane didn't want to come. But I can tell by her voice that she's thrilled to be on her own. When I turned down my Walkman for a minute, I heard Pit telling Mom about how drumming puts her in touch with her "earth energy" and Geraldine agreeing that drumming loosened her "lower chakras." It's hard to tell whether it is loosened earth energy or just B.O. and patchouli smelling up the car.

I talked to George last night before we left. She told me about this aunt of hers who grew up in the bush ouside of Houston and went away to school in the city to study religion. She fell in with the animal rights people and somehow got the idea that she had to repent for the traplines she ran to make money. When George's aunt finally moved back to Houston, she made a huge fake trap out of cardboard and tin foil and mounted it on the top of her car, an old beater Toyota. She painted the words "Death Trap" in dripping red letters on both sides of the car. Sometimes George has to get a ride to school with her aunt! In the Death Trap! Can you imagine? That's even more embarrassing than driving around with Pit and Geraldine in our car. George thinks that the trauma of having a Death Trap aunt has played a central role in making Eugene and Bone so insecure.

Hearing George's story made me feel better somehow. I was also impressed that she has such interesting, if demented, relatives.

I think MacGregor is a bit concerned about the fish. He put them into three plastic bags with water, and we stopped at the hardware-pet store on the way out of town and had the clerk put some pure oxygen in the plastic bags. His fish expert told him that's how fish are shipped long distances. The oxygen lets the fish stay alive in the bags longer. It's kind of like putting the fish in a hyperbaric chamber, if you think about it. The problem is that now the fish are acting like hopped-up athletes.

MacGregor has the bags in a bucket at his feet, and he keeps leaning in to see if there have been any casualties yet. It was probably a mistake to put the mutant angelfish pair in one bag together. They are out of control at the best of times. Now, aided by a shot of pure oxygen, they are totally manic. I hope the fish-show judges are partial to shredded fins and missing eyes. The betta is in full display. He is pretty spectacular to begin with. Now his flowing red fins are all extended and he seems to be trying to catch the eye of one of the baby angels in the bag next to his. The little angelfish are racing back and forth and doing little dashes at one another, at least as much as they can in the confines of a plastic bag.

I would offer some advice to MacGregor on how to deal with the situation, but I have to keep my headphones on so as not to hear the hippie horrors from up front.

Later

We are still not there. It will be a miracle if we reach Terrace alive. My mother doesn't speed or anything like that, but her driving style is extremely erratic. She's afraid of the big trucks. If one gets behind us, she slows the car to a crawl and tries to find somewhere to pull over. This is a problem because there are about two places on the way to Terrace with enough room on the shoulder to let someone pass. So we are inching along Highway 16 at about fifty kilometers an hour with all these big rigs and other vehicles backed up behind us. If this were the United States, some driver with road rage would have shot Mom long ago.

She also does this crazy veering thing whenever a semi comes toward us. Most of the road to Terrace has a towering cliff with falling-rock warnings on one side and a raging river on the other side, with the narrow little two-lane highway running between. There isn't anywhere to swerve to, but somehow she manages. It is amazing to watch. In addition to swerving the car itself, she also sort of ducks her body. All very confidence inspiring.

Still Later

Apparently Pit also finds Mother's driving stressful. When Mom finally found a rest stop to pull into, it took about ten minutes for all the traffic backed up behind us to go by. The looks we got were murderous. Even the blue-haired ladies and hat-wearing old men in monster motor homes shook their fists at us. God.

Anyhow, when I came back from the washroom, Pit was in the driver's seat. This should be interesting. Pit strikes me as one of those confident people with bad judgment. I bet she's a terrifying driver.

Pit is out of control. She keeps saying how driving makes her feel "so free" and puts her in touch with her "goddess energy." I guess race-car drivers must have goddess energy to burn, because it seems to result in extreme speed.

We are careening all over the road, and I bet we've passed every single car that was backed up behind us when Mom was at the wheel. The terror is so bad that I have had to take my headphones off to concentrate better on praying.

Pit is passing people on hairpin turns, for God's sake. Everyone in the car has stopped talking. We are all pressed into our seats and clutching the dash or door handles. It's going to take the Jaws of Life to get Mom's hands off the dashboard.

But old Pit, she's not even noticing the waves of fear coming off her passengers. The fact that our car is doing 140 kilometers an hour in a 90-kilometer zone isn't fazing her at all. The fact that even the slightest dip in the road makes us airborne has also escaped her attention. She's going on about how in her Letting Go ceremony last week she had this big insight into her need for security, and after burning some sage and doing the Dance of Life or something, she's ready to live without fear. Just my luck. She decides to give up on healthy fear and now she's driving our car. I'll tell you, my need to hold on is about a thousand times stronger since Pit started driving. All the New Age rituals in the world aren't going to get me over this trauma. I am going to need intensive, long-term therapy to deal with this. I'm probably scarred forever. I'll probably have to walk everywhere because Pit has induced an incapacitating phobia about vehicles in me.

Even MacGregor's fish have gone as still as they can in the plastic bags, which are sloshing around like water balloons at a birthday party. My writing is all over the page. But I can't let this moment pass undocumented. This notebook may end up being like the little black box in a plane crash. People are going to want to know what could possibly have happened that we had to go this fast to a fish show.

Can't we ever have a normal family outing? The only blessing I can see is that Pit has probably shaved about an hour off the trip.

Later, but not late

What an entrance! Of course we had an accident as soon as we pulled into the Terrace Community Center parking lot doing about 80 kilometers per hour. A crash was inevitable. I'm just glad that no one, well, no one except for Geraldine, got hurt. I think Geraldine's injury is a bit of a load anyway. After all, Pit just nicked the end of that trailer. It crumpled and jackknifed as we hit it, and Pit slammed on the brakes at the end of the parking lot and put her hand up to her mouth.

"Oh wow. Did I just hit something?"

Mom unclenched her jaws and said: "Yes. Yes, you did hit something."

Geraldine spoke up:

"Oh, my neck! It's wrenched."

Mom snarled at her: "It is not."

Then she turned to Pit.

"Do you always drive like that? For God's sake, that was the most terrifying experience of my life! Our insurance is going to go through the roof. My children are in the car. Jesus H. Christ."

I couldn't help but notice our placement in my mother's list of concerns, but decided not to remark on it just at that moment.

Pit responded: "Oh wow. I'm really sorry."

A small bristly-mustached man stormed over to the car. His face was red and his mouth frothed as he screamed: "What in the hell tarnation was that? You hit ma trailer! You hit ma freakin' trailer!"

He was wearing combat fatigues and had a bowie knife in a belt at his waist.

Pit gingerly rolled down the window.

"Was that your trailer?" she asked.

"What the freakin' hell do you think?" he shrieked. "A course it's ma freakin' trailer. And a good thing for you, lady, I got my fish outa there afore you hit it. Two minutes earlier and you'da taken out a thousand dollars' worth of killies!" As an afterthought he added,

"And my wife, too. If she'da been in there, she coulda been injured." Only the way he said it sounded like "inured."

Pit kept apologizing, and Mom and Geraldine and I staggered out of the car, our fear-sick legs buckling as we tried to use them.

MacGregor leaned over to the front seat.

"You brought killies to the show?" he asked.

The enraged little man peered in at MacGregor, who sat gripping his bucket of hopped-up, traumatized fish between his knees and said, "Yeah. I brung a bunch of killies to the show and auction. Got the dried eggs too. How 'bout you? Whatcha got there?"

Pit, Mom, Geraldine, and I stood in a little huddle off to the side waiting for our knees to stop shaking as MacGregor and Mustache talked fish. Apparently killies are some type of seasonal, just-add-water type fish, and the little man was the foremost breeder in the country or something. He, in turn, was supplied by another top breeder who lives in a compound in Montana, which is where he was originally from.

Deep in conversation, MacGregor and "Call me Pete. Yeah, I been working on the German Chocolate killie strain for two years now" walked past us into the community center. Pete paused briefly to glower at Pit and tell her he'd be back for her insurance information later.

Pit and Geraldine got their drums out of the car, and Mom and I followed MacGregor and Pete into the gym.

Thank God for MacGregor and his fish. If it had just

been stinky Geraldine and Hairy Pit, I think Pete would have used that bowie knife. An American in combat gear at a fish show is not someone to be messed with. Pete's probably one of those militia guys who're waiting for the end to come so they can revert to their preferred diet of squirrels. Those killies sure sound like the ultimate sur-vivalist fish.

The gym had a stage set up at one end and plastic chairs in rows facing it. In the back half of the gym about fifteen tables were set up. On each table sat several fish bowls or small tanks. Behind the fish containers sat the proud owners and breeders.

MacGregor stood over by Pete's table. Pete had a table all to himself with about twenty bowls on top, each con-taining a little fish or pair of fish. A downtrodden, fish-hating-looking woman who must have been Pete's wife, the one who barely missed being "inured," was slumped behind the table. There were at least two other militia-type guys, one standing behind some fancy guppies and one behind a bowl of tiny, darting cardinal tetras.

The other people showing off their finned prizes were a motley assortment, even by northern British Columbia standards. There were some intense-looking children and a few bored-looking children with intense parents, a couple of bikers in leather and tattoos and scars, a 4-H fish contingent, and some earnest scientific types, whose bowls and tanks were obscured by pipes and tubes and other odd filtration arrangements.

MacGregor found the table he had been assigned, and Mom and I helped him get set up. Mom wanted to make his area special and homey, so she put a woven cloth runner under his three bowls, but a fish official came by and made us remove it because it was unfair to the other fish. MacGregor transferred his fish from their bags into bowls. He polished the bowls to a shine and deftly removed a bit of poop hanging down from the betta with some tweezers, a tip he'd picked up on the Internet. Then he set up their little placards. *Betta splendens*–male, unmated. *Pterophyllum scalare*–mated pair. *Pterophyllum scalare*–juveniles, unsexed.

It was all pretty exciting, I have to admit. I could feel hereditary competitiveness begin to wash over me. I forgot about the whole objectification-of-fish-protest thing and got swept up in the magic of the precompetition moment. MacGregor's shining cheeks, his cords, his boots, and his fishbowls were too beautiful to criticize. In spite of my familial will to win, I found the other contestants (the owners, not the fish) kind of cool, too, as they futzed around with their show animals, completely oblivious to how weird they were. The contestants walked around asking each other earnest questions and praising each other freely.

A curly-haired, apple-cheeked, glowing-with-health young man appeared at our table and was soon talking earnestly with MacGregor and shaking our hands.

"Great to see you, Mac. Glad you could make it."

Polite, friendly, he couldn't have been nicer. After

greeting me and my mom with gentle sincerity, he began introducing MacGregor around.

"Hi, Chuck. This is MacGregor MacLeod. We could learn some things from his approach. Good, solid fish-keeping skills . . ."

Conversations hummed around the gymnasium.

"So that's a great-looking oscar. He chase everyone else out of your tank?"

"I've never seen a rasbora that size. What are you feeding?"

"Tell me about this German filtration system. I read about it in *The Freshwater Aquarist News*, but this is the first time I've ever seen one."

Mom and I joined MacGregor and Colin, the curly-haired young man, on their socializing rounds. We read other people's placards, and MacGregor asked a few questions. No one seemed to notice that he was only ten years old. It was really something to see him having a heart-to-heart about betta constipation with a drop-dead beautiful 4-H girl, and talking fin fray with a three-hundred-pound biker. One stuffy cardigan-wearing man was a bit condescending when MacGregor asked him whether his discus weren't too delicate to show, but Mom, who is not always uncool, looked closely at the man's fish and asked him if hole-in-the-head disease would make a difference in the judging. Colin, the Ken Doll of the fish world, quickly hid his smile behind his hand. The man sputtered and my mother strode away.

We eventually settled down behind MacGregor's fish, and Mom hauled out the lunch basket. MacGregor was off having some groundbreaking conversation about the finer points of the biotope aquarium, so Mom made me take Pit and Geraldine their lunches.

"I don't know where the drumming room is."

"Just follow the noise."

"More like follow the smell," I muttered.

"Alice, you promised to be civilized. We are here to help MacGregor. This is his day. So help."

"Yeesh."

She was distracted again. "And take a sandwich with you. You know how you get when you don't eat."

I shot her a glare that she was too busy being competitive to notice.

As soon as I got out of the gym, I ditched my sandwich in a garbage bin and headed off through the Terrace Community Center. The people hanging around looked just as frumpy as the ones who hang out at the community center in Smithers. I put my headphones on so none of them would try to engage me in conversation. I stopped to look at some photos of local sports heroes in the hallway. One soccer player had a mustache drawn on him and the word *prick* written in crayon underneath. It made me want to check out the washrooms to find out who was considered the slut in town. Who can fail to appreciate passion and honesty wherever they appear?

The truth is, I was dawdling. I really don't care for Geraldine and Pit, and in fact was worried that I might

214

actually be allergic to them. The thought of bringing them their lunches as though I somehow wanted to help them in their pursuit of increased emotional and physical messiness, well, it was almost more than I could bear.

The drumming workshop was announced down the hall by the smell of incense and the degenerate rhythms of the various drummers. As luck would have it, I got to the door just as they were about to take a break. That foiled my plan of dropping the lunch bags outside the door with "For Geraldine and Friend" written on them. I couldn't bring myself to call Pit anything but Pit, and even I don't think that is an appropriate name to put on her lunch bag.

I could tell Pit and Geraldine were in their glory. Everywhere they looked, they saw their fashion sense and value system reflected back at them.

Everyone at the workshop had long hair and badly maintained cotton clothing. There were middle-aged women obviously in the throes of a midlife crisis and some disgruntled government employee-looking men, dressed conservatively but with a statement feature, like a rattail or moccasins. They all looked shyly proud to be in the company of such countercultural (if passé) people as Pit and Geraldine and the drum workshop leader guy.

When I walked in, Pit and Geraldine made a big show of how "groovy" it was to see me. I pretended that I couldn't hear them and just held up their lunches. The leader, a sock-and-sandal-wearing bearded type, decided that I represented the perfect opportunity to educate the drummers on the excitement of introducing rhythms to the repressed.

"Welcome. Welcome," he boomed as he strolled over.

I pretended that I couldn't hear because I was listening to my headphones. I bobbed my head a bit and furtively eyed the door. Before I could get away, Jesus of Terrace and Pit and Geraldine had me cornered and were standing in a semicircle around me.

"You know what is so cool?" said Jesus, gesturing for me to take off my headphones, while the whole class stared at me with that dumb, openly welcoming look on their faces.

"The ability drums have to bring people together," he continued.

I was beginning to get this paranoid feeling they had been talking about me before I showed up.

Jesus turned to me.

"How would you like to join us for a jam?"

If he had been much heartier, he would have hurt him-self. Everyone was staring at me. I couldn't pretend not to hear.

Before I knew it, he had me sitting in the middle of the room on a low stool with a big drum between my knees. He sat facing me, and the rest of the class sat in a circle around us.

Now, apparently going for a look of intuitive intensity, with a lot of long pauses between eyelid blinks, Jesus of Terrace told me to follow his lead. I, cowardly worm that I am, did. He began hitting the drum with this vaguely obscene soft slap. I, head retreating into my shoulders, did the same. It made my stomach curl and soften. Jesus picked up the pace and I followed. All the time he stared at me, bug-eyed.

Jesus gave the sheep the sign, and they all began to join in. The sound was almost visible. It got louder and louder. Some of the more susceptible types began to sway. They all stared at me. And the really sick thing was that I was starting to get into it. I was moving back and forth a bit on my stool, and my hands were following the rhythm almost against my will. It was pure voodoo. People began breaking off into their own rhythms, my shoulders began doing this boogie-dip thing, and my head was bobbing up and down. Powerless. I was powerless over the beat.

When it was finally over, I felt shame, sickening shame, at how easily influenced I am. Why am I always liking things I'm supposed to hate? The drummers all clapped, and I nodded a bit and grabbed my huge headphones and ducked out of the room. I guess it was just another example of my lack of character, my lack of personal integrity and strength, my overwhelming weakness. I'm never going to make it as a cultural critic if I keep liking the worst things our culture has to offer (*Buffy* not included, of course).

When I got back to the fish show, the judging was underway. The judges were a group of three middle-aged men. They wore dress shirts and shiny slacks, and one of them was seriously overweight. They moved as a unit, from one fish container to the next.

The fish owners squirmed and answered the questions put to them by the judges. The judges—Bill, Jim, and Randy, according to their name tags—made no effort to put the contestants at ease. Even the militia members seemed quiet and submissive.

I could see Mom beginning to deconstruct a bit as the judges neared our table. Her competitiveness made her body twitch and her eyes bulge as she peered over at the competition. As the judges looked at our tablemate's show fish—a vicious-looking black veil tail with what appeared to be a bit of fin sticking out of his mouth, suggesting that he used to be one of a pair—Mom put on her best Confident Mother of Successful Children look. Bill, Jim, and Randy stopped in front of MacGregor's betta bowl first.

"Hmmm," they said.

MacGregor looked up at them. Mom, ambition leaking from every seam, asked if they needed any "background on the fish?"

Fat Randy declined her offer, and Bill and Jim gave her a disapproving look. Mom smiled at them gauntly, like a starving she-wolf, as Randy and Bill and Jim moved along to purse their lips at MacGregor's pair of angelfish.

"Hmmm," they said, with slightly more inflection this time, or so it seemed to my ears. They looked back and forth from the angels to their fry for a few minutes. I could see Mom struggling to control herself. MacGregor, interested but unconcerned, watched the judges watch his fish. When the judges asked the age of the fry, MacGregor answered truthfully. The little flotilla of judges moved off, and my mother, exhausted, slumped back into her chair for a moment before beginning to whisper furiously at me about the nuances she had picked up in "hmmm." She was convinced that the question about the fry was really significant.

My mother is a lunatic. The stress was too much, and I was forced to go outside. Watching her in the throes of maternal competitiveness was awful. I know that she is only rarely able to indulge it. After all, so far I am not a winner in any area of life. In fact I am not even in the game, for the most part, and MacGregor, being young, hardly ever enters the playing field. I am sure that when he's won a Nobel prize for his work on behalf of fish everywhere, Mom will be able to sit back and relax, but until then she can't resist the urge to help.

Wanting to be proud of one's offspring is a sickness. I wish I could help my mother with her sense of self-worth via my own success, I really do. I just don't see any parental pride-making activities or events in my future.

Later

I was sitting outside the community center beside the cross-country track, staring at page thirty-five of *The Fellowship of the Ring* when he jogged by. At first he looked like a normal jogger. But as he got closer, I realized there was something strange about the way he moved.

The cross-country track is a dirt path about two miles long that goes around the community center, back into the trees, and around behind the police station. According to legend, school officials once tried to hold an Alternative Schools Sports Day in Terrace. The organizers had the students run the cross-country path. Of course the Smithers behavior cases met the Terrace behavior cases, and instantly the trail was littered with truants in trees, smoking pot and planning small-scale break-and-enter jobs. The teachers got in a lot of trouble, and that cross-country run was the first and final event of the one and only Annual Sports Day. I'm just surprised it wasn't worse. I bet there are still Alternative cases lurking around the track, sort of like Vietnam vets who don't know that the war is over. Apparently several kids didn't get back on the bus when the Smithers juvenile delinquents were shipped back in disgrace.

Anyway, when he jogged by on the root-studded running path, I couldn't help but notice that he didn't look very athletic. His hair looked like he'd been at it with the nail scissors. He wore a threadbare yellow T-shirt. His stride was strange—the steps too long and high, his arms shooting out in all directions. It looked more like the flapping of a small goose than a workout. As he got closer, I realized that it wasn't just his running form that was bizarre. His shoes were peculiar too. Baggy pants pulled up past his ankles to show that he was wearing big yellow leather work boots, their tongues and laces slapping around as he charged by.

As he ran past me, he looked over with open interest on his small face. He smiled broadly and then, incredibly, leaped onto a post set in the ground to mark the entrance to the running path. One work boot landed heavily on the post, and he kicked out his other foot, wrenched his head around to look at me again, and then crashed off down the path.

He was great. I couldn't believe it was possible to be so unself-conscious. My God, who was this Gooseboy? He was everything I wanted and everything I'm not.

In a turmoil, an inner frenzy, I stayed seated beside the running path. Should I stay? Should I go? Would he come around again? Was he doing laps? Was it possible to do laps in boots like that? Would he be tripped up on a root or a rock, injured, and I would never see him again?

I sat, practically writhing in an agony of nerves, and said a silent prayer of thanks that I was wearing all my best Prince George thrift finds. I straightened my headphones, pulled down my lime velour stretch top, smoothed my red-and-white-checked pants, rearranged my silver vest, fixed my barrettes, and wondered if he would notice me. I imagined seeing him again. I would say something meaningful that would let him know that I saw him clearly and appreciated him. Or better yet, I would just show him that I was a kindred spirit.

Maybe I could get myself some oddball workout gear and meet him on the path. I could wear billowing parachute pants or short shorts and striped knee-high socks, and a big old overcoat with a cheap tiara perched on my great hair, and maybe some red patent pumps. I could struggle along the path, doing a run-sashay type thing, tripping and falling every few feet, but bravely picking myself up, and wiping off my tiara and placing it carefully back on my head each time. I would stage a big fall as I passed him, and he would grind to a stop and gallantly use his cruddy yellow T-shirt to mop the blood oozing from my knees.

I was quite choked up just from imagining it. Of course, I had quite a bit of time to fantasize since the path was long and the boy did not seem to be going very fast. In fact, with all that time to think, I began to wonder if my intense interest in boys was becoming, like, a pattern or something? I mean, first Aubrey and now this. I am only fifteen. It all seemed a bit, well, unseemly. Perhaps, and I cringed to think it, I was becoming some kind of tart. One of those girls who want to know how to get and keep a guy, who want to know what guys think looks good on them and take tests to find out if their personality makes them girlfriend material. Well, at least I can spare myself the ordeal of a whole battery of personality tests. My personality is poor; that much is clear.

Caught up in my horrible thoughts of how I was turning into some kind of needy floozy, I didn't see Gooseboy's second approach. I looked up when I heard the snapping and whipping sounds of his leather boot laces. He grinned, his nose a surprised punctuation point between his mouth and eyes. I could feel the stupid look fall across my face.

He came closer, hitting the ground so hard that it shook with each footstep. He came closer still, until he was just opposite, huge grin still trained on me. For a second it looked as though he might keep going. He wind-milled along for about another meter or so, momentum propelling him past the spot where I was sitting. Finally he got his limbs under control and pulled up and, with movements at least as spastic as his run, flailed around to face me.

What an incredible-looking boy. He had even, white teeth made brighter by what looked like a dirt mustache beneath his nose. And I, overwhelmed, outside myself, spoke first.

"Hi."

His grin got even bigger.

"Hi," he said.

"Running, huh?" I said brilliantly, still too captivated by his teeth to let my self-consciousness drive me back inside myself.

"Oh. Yeah," he said. "You?"

"What do you mean?" I asked.

The smile dimmed a bit and he replied to his own question.

"Yeah. Duh. Of course you aren't running. I can see that. You're reading a book."

I looked down at my hand and was surprised to see *Fellowship* in it.

His hair was blond and so straight it came off his head at right angles, except on one side where it stuck flat to his head like he'd been sleeping on it.

"So . . ."

"Yeah," he said, and hunched his small shoulders a bit, and then kicked an invisible rock on the ground with his scuffed work boot. Oh man, I was lost.

He was a hands-in-pockets rock kicker.

"Live around here?" he asked.

"No. Not really. Smithers."

"Yeah?"

"Uh-huh," I replied.

He was showing signs of shyness, rocking back and forth and squirming a bit, but when he looked at me, it was full on.

"My brother's in the fish show here." I gestured back at the community center with my hand.

"Get out!" he crowed, breaking into another huge grin. "Me too."

I took a step back. My heart sank.

He was fishy. Of all the luck.

"I mean, mine too!" He beamed like he'd accomplished something. "In fact, my brother practically put this thing on."

Gooseboy laughed heartily like he couldn't quite believe it, and in that second I saw the resemblance.

"A fish show! Isn't that great!" he continued.

"Which one is your brother?" I asked, already know-ing the answer.

"Colin. Colin Feckworth."

I couldn't believe it. This was MacGregor's mentor's brother.

"Shouldn't you be in there?" I gestured back at the community center.

"Oh, no. I'm not showing. I don't have fish. I'm not very good with pets. I'm basically bad at anything you have to remember to feed."

Relief washed over me.

I couldn't think of anything to say, so I pointed at his face and said, "I think you have some dirt on your lip."

And couldn't believe I had said it the second it left my mouth.

But Goose wasn't fazed at all.

"Har!" he bellowed, and rubbed his hair. "You mean my mustache!" He looked strangely pleased.

"It's pretty new," he explained. "I'm trying to, you know, encourage it, so I don't want to disturb it by shaving or anything."

"Maybe you have to shave it once to get it started?" I suggested, remembering what my mom had once told me about why some women don't shave their thighs. Not wanting to go down that road, I changed the subject.

"You from here?" I asked.

"Nope. Rupert. I got a ride down here with my

brother. This friend of mine was supposed to be playing hockey here, but I guess I got the day wrong or something."

"Really?" I said, actually interested, even though I'm normally not interested in the stuff people have to say about themselves. Unless, of course, they aren't talking to me. But every word Gooseboy said was fascinating.

"Yeah," he said, sighing heavily and rubbing his head some more. "I get things wrong a lot. My friend Rod, the one I was coming to see, he's a great player. Not like me. I played hockey for a while, but I kept getting left staring into space at the wrong end of the play. Coach said I wasn't alert enough–figured I was going to get hurt.

"Actually," he continued, "I've been experimenting, and I don't appear to be good at anything."

His head rubbing became thoughtful.

"Yup. Not good at team sports really, or math, or video games, or Rollerblading. Or woodworking. So I'm trying cross-country running to see if I might be good at that."

I felt compelled to help.

"Well, I bet you'd be faster if you wore better shoes. Those boots are probably too heavy for running."

He looked down at his boots with a quizzical look on his face.

"You think so? You're probably right. I just don't want to spend the money on new shoes till I'm sure I've got a future in running."

"Uh, right," I said.

"Because money's one thing I'm okay with. I've been buying my own clothes since I was like seven or eight years old or something. Trick to saving money on clothes is never buy new." He said this with great sincerity.

I nodded, entranced, and wondered if he'd bought the huge flood pants he was wearing on one of his earlier shopping trips by himself.

He cast a look and me and ventured a conspiratorial guess. "You buy your own too, eh?"

I laughed out loud. I couldn't help it. I wondered if Goose knew that everybody our age bought their own clothes. Maybe his brother was too scientific to be bothered. I know MacGregor is, but he's just ten.

We stood there, me laughing at him and him just laughing.

"Want to go in?" I asked.

"Sure," he said.

So we walked back to the fish show in silence. He was sort of sweaty, like he'd been jogging for miles in yellow leather work boots. I looked like I always do, but I carried my headphones, so as not to miss it if he said something. I figure anyone watching would have known we were allowed to buy our own clothes.

When we walked into the gym, the judges were in the middle of announcing the prizes. The largest judge, Randy, was at the microphone. He was saying how the category of finest killie fish in the show had been a difficult call and that the caliber of the competition was "absolutely top-notch." And then he called Pete up to collect first, second, and third prize for best killies in the show. Pete's wife, still slumped behind the array of killie containers, raised one eyebrow and clapped in a dispirited, this-will-just-encourage-him way.

The next category was for best breeding pair and fry. Randy blathered on about how essential it was to reproduce the good characteristics of the parents and so on. From where we stood at the back of the gym, I could see my mother staring with a psychotic intensity at Fat Randy while she clutched MacGregor's hand. I am pretty sure I saw MacGregor wince. Mom's competitiveness really is bordering on child abuse.

Randy paused for dramatic effect after his tension-building spiel and then announced:

"And the first prize for best breeding pair goes to MacGregor MacLeod and his lovely pair of angelfish."

My mother screamed and leaped up, banging into the table and slopping water from the fishbowls all over the place. The other contestants shot her looks of intense dislike. MacGregor, small and pleased, stood up and went to get his big blue ribbon. I grabbed the hand of Gooseboy and whispered, "That's my brother."

He, impressed, said, "Really?" and to show he understood, added, "He must have really nice fish."

He was perfect. And even though he was a bit sweaty and everything, he still smelled kind of good. Not like flowers or anything, but manly somehow.

Carried away, I grabbed his hand again and repeated, "Yup. That's my brother."

He got into the spirit of the moment, and keeping a grip on my hand, pointed with his free hand at Colin, who stood off to the side looking wholesome and competent.

"And that's mine!"

I glanced over to see my mother staring at me, mouth hanging open, and I quickly dropped Goose's hand. MacGregor was up on the stage with the judges, shaking their hands and collecting his ribbon.

It was the best of times, it was the worst of times. I mean really, I was just a bit overtaxed by the whole thing—my positive feelings for the talentless (except at dressing badly and making me laugh) Gooseboy, my pride in MacGregor—all of it. It was that bloody drumming session that did it, I bet. It loosened up that nice, warm vibe part of me or something. After the whole Frank thing, I had pretty much decided to write off people, even the rare cool ones, but here I was.

I was overwhelmed by sappiness and irritation. Why was my mother always around when I met someone? Why did she get to see it? I have a friend now. Why couldn't I have been out with George when I realized I have an attraction to my brother's fish mentor's brother?

I felt this peculiar sensation. I think it was the woman-hood tent beckoning. Just standing near the sweaty Gooseboy was making me feel completely squishy. It was horrible! I had enough problems without adding squishi-ness to the equation. Totally.

Goose, being very cool, was displaying only mild interest in the fish show. I wondered if he thought about the womanhood tent when he looked at me. It wasn't impossible. I mean, I thought those red-and-white-checked stretch pants looked pretty good. And they hardly cost anything.

I found myself gazing at him again. And then turned to catch my mother staring at me with total incomprehension. On the other side Gooseboy's brother stood, staring at us too, his face a mirror of my mother's confusion.

Then my mother grabbed the disposable fun camera with flash and started snapping shots as MacGregor came down the steps from the stage, beaming shyly and clutching his big ribbon. Colin moved in to congratulate him.

A voice came over the intercom announcing a break before the auction started.

While Mom and Colin were distracted with MacGregor and his award, I grabbed Goose's hand and asked him if he wanted to go for a walk. He shrugged amiably and said, "Sure." We walked along the back of the gym and out the big double doors.

We stood outside the gym in the hallway and sort of smiled at each other sideways, deciding what to do.

Then it hit me. I knew what we could do. We could go to the womanhood tent. I mean, I had achieved practically every single Life Goal a person my age could be expected to attempt, excluding an essay on chicken peer groups that the local library doesn't have the resources to support. It was time for some sex! It briefly occurred to me to wonder if Gooseboy was ready for it, but I dismissed the thought. He was experimenting, after all. Who knows, sex might just be his area of expertise or something. It couldn't be that much harder than finding cheap clothes.

I looked into his face.

"How about we find somewhere to sit down?" I asked, racking my brain for the right sort of setting for a Terrace Community Center seduction.

"Uh, okay," he said, and then gave me an intent look. "What are you thinking?"

"Oh, you know, maybe we could just find somewhere to, you know, sit down."

"You mean like in the hall?"

"No, more of a private-type place."

His eyebrows shot up.

"Get out of here!" he almost yelled.

"What?" I asked, startled.

"Are you, like . . ." he trailed off. "Are you wanting to, you know, hang out privately?" he asked, incredulous, his eyebrows hidden in his scalp.

Embarrassment washed over me and I scowled at him and said nothing.

"I mean, you want to be, or go somewhere with me?" he continued. And then, and I couldn't quite believe it, he did a little jiggy dance right on the spot. He was not a good dancer, but it was one of the funnier things I've ever seen.

"Oh man. Oh man! Okay! Let's go!" He grabbed my hand and we headed down the hall.

We walked quickly, briefly discussing our options.

The pottery room? No, the tables were too high. The staff lounge? Maybe, but it was probably a bit too populated. As we passed each room, we ruled it out for one reason or another. It was an adventure and we didn't have time to get nervous. Then we walked past the day-care room. It had a little cloakroom at the side, with an undersized sofa sectional in the corner, probably for the parents to sit in as they dressed their kids to go outside. It was perfect.

"What do you think?" he whispered.

"I don't know. Seems okay." I shrugged.

We tiptoed into the cloakroom and closed the day-care door, with its appealingly low handle, behind us. I went and sat on one half of the little right-angles couch. The sofa crouched low to the ground, and as I sat on it, my knees felt like they were up around my ears.

Now Goose was starting to look a bit awkward. He stood in the middle of the cloakroom like he wasn't sure where to put himself.

As he was going for the lights, I quickly said, "Why don't you leave them off and come sit down?"

I gestured at the other piece of the sofa. Then I trapped my hands between my knees to stop them from shaking with the pretent jitters.

What was I doing? This was lunacy, even for me. I mean, I know that boy-girl interaction was on my list, but I suspect this wasn't what Mrs. Freison meant by a maturity indicator. Or maybe this was exactly what she meant. I was well-read enough to know about sex, and my mother's embarrassing legacy of openness had left me with few illusions about the mechanics of it. But up until now I hadn't had any interest in the proceedings, except for Frank's inspiring example on that trail ride. Damn drumming. If religious groups want to keep their young people from having sex until they are married, I strongly suggest getting rid of the drums in the school band. I was feeling this attraction and detachment, sort of an I-feel-squishy-and-besides-I-might-as-well-get-this-over-with type of feeling.

Poor Goose. He paced back and forth a few times, a small person in large boots, and then came and sat down on the little flowered sofa. He stuck his hands under his thighs and started drumming his steel toes against the floor. And every time he made a nervous gesture, I felt more confident.

I watched him out of the corner of my eye as he glared into space, obviously psyching himself up. I was surprised he didn't give himself a pep talk right in front of me.

"You can sit a bit closer if you want."

"Okay. Yeah. Sounds good." He maneuvered himself up and over. Then he put his hands on his knees and continued tapping his boots on the floor.

When he was settled, uncomfortably, beside me, I twisted myself around and sort of thrust my arm behind him. There was hardly any room to move, and the child-sized sofa's springs didn't have the strength to support us, so we slowly sank toward the floor. The couch must have been hell for parents to sit on, even just to zip up jackets and put on little boots. For the two of us about to engage in intimacy, it was torture.

My arm immediately went numb and Gooseboy's face went bright red, but catching the spirit of the thing, he lifted his arm and put it around my shoulders. Every time we took a breath, my silver vest made a noise like a hundred cello-phane packages being crumpled. It was distracting, but I was determined, so I squeezed my eyes shut and turned my face up to wait for the wash of passion to surge over me.

Nothing happened.

When I opened my eyes again, he was peering into them.

"Can I kiss you?" he asked.

I wondered briefly if Frank had this problem with her conquests.

"Um. Yeah," I said.

So he kissed me. You can't imagine how bizarre it felt. Somebody else's lips were actually touching mine. My neck ached and my nose was filled with his smell, and my trapped arm shook uncontrollably from lack of blood, but I was kissing.

It didn't take long before the kissing became boring. There really would have had to be a lot of action going on to keep us distracted from the pain of being on that couch. I guess you could say it was the pain and not the passion spurring us on.

Gooseboy wasn't exactly taking the bull by the horns, so I decided to help him out a bit. I grabbed his hand, the one that wasn't squashed behind me, digging into my spasming, twisted back, and put it under my vest. Like a creature with a small, slow brain of its own, his hand froze for a minute and then, startled, flew off my chest.

I replaced it. This time the hand stayed where I put it, although it seemed sort of uncertain about what to do. First it didn't move. Then it kind of wandered back and forth and up and down, just sliding around without any master plan. Even though the hand seemed somewhat clueless about feeling me up, it had the effect of making me feel even squishier, and the pain of the cloakroom couch receded a bit.

So far Goose wasn't showing much natural talent in the intimacy arena, but maybe with practice he could improve. I decided to make a definitive move. I took the hand from where it was doing laps and, perhaps a bit unceremoniously, stuck it, well, farther south. The hand froze.

All the while, we continued to kiss.

My mother's sex education books hadn't really covered much except for my growing woman's body and what was supposed to feel good for me. I didn't have a clue what I was supposed to do with him and his body.

The hand remained immobilized where I had placed it. It tried sneaking down towards my knee. I knew that was the wrong direction, so I gave it a bit of a push, like you would push a kid on a swing, back and forth and back again as it retreated. The hand obeyed, although reluctantly, it seemed to me. Gradually the hand didn't need to be pushed and the pain of the couch was forgotten.

All-consuming squishiness.

At least until my mother, somewhat predictably, burst through the door and threw on the lights. She was followed by Pete's wife, who looked relieved to get away from the fish, even for such a sordid encounter as this.

Gooseboy shot up as though electrified, knocking me to the floor. Then, realizing what he had done, he abruptly stooped down to help me up, but I was already on my way up and our heads knocked together, making a sound that signaled thick, sickening pain to come. I dropped back to my hands and knees, and Gooseboy reeled off to one side of the cloakroom.

My mother and Pete's increasingly happy-looking wife stood there staring as I tried to focus on the floor and ignore my overwhelming desire to throw up. Gooseboy grabbed at his head and adjusted his twisted-up flood pants at the same time. Finally I sat back on my heels, holding on to my head with both hands. I looked up at the crowd of spectators and wondered what Frank would have said. I came up with:

"What are you staring at?"

It was not a statement calculated to calm my mother, who was obviously deciding whether she was going to be hysterically angry or just hysterical.

"What am I looking at?" she asked in a voice tight enough to choke. "What the hell am I looking at? What the hell do you think I'm looking at!"

She turned and faced Goose.

"Who are you?"

And to me: "Who is he? Where did you get him?"

Then she really got going.

"Do you really think this is appropriate? Huh? How could you do this to me after all I went through with Frank? What possessed you to think this is an appropriate place for a . . ." She faltered, looking for the right word. "First date?" she finished.

Pete's wife stood beside her, thrilled and beaming but trying to look supportively disapproving.

Gooseboy, having gathered up his manners, stuck out his hand to my mother, his head retreating so far into his shoulders that his neck was only a theory, and said, "Oh. Hi. I'm Daniel Feckworth. My brother's with the fish show."

Mom stared at him blankly for a second.

"Who?"

"Oh, my brother, Colin, he's with the fish show. You know, he sort of put it on. And I was waiting for him. Well, actually I was sort of running, and then I met . . ."

His voice trailed off when he realized he didn't know my name.

"Alice," I prompted sullenly from the floor.

"Right. Alice. And we were just kind of talking, you know. About you know, um, things. And then we decided to . . ."

She cut him off.

"I can see what you decided. My God, Alice. Are you trying to kill me?"

I didn't think that deserved an answer.

"Well, the auction is supposed to start soon," my mother huffed. She looked at Gooseboy.

"I'm sure you have something to do." And to me: "And you, come with me."

I didn't look up and continued to train my scowl at the floor.

Pete's wife commented that I really had an "attitude problem," and I could tell that Mom was torn between defending me to the outsider and killing me. Finally Mom pointed down at me with a shaking index finger. "I am going back to get MacGregor, and you had better meet us in that gym in five minutes."

Then she turned, banging into a child-size plastic picnic table. She reluctantly accepted steadying by Pete's wife and slammed out the door.

We stayed rooted in our spots until long after my mother left, echoes of her trailing down the hall and disappearing into the gym. I finally moved so I was sitting with my back against the couch, keeping my eyes on the floor in front of me. Daniel/Gooseboy shuffled around and continued to rub his head.

"So," he said, "I'm really, um, sorry about this."

I, sickened by the thought of discussing what had just happened, got even more involved in my study of the floor.

He continued. "It was really nice to meet you."

Silence rang around the cloakroom.

"So. Do you think I could call you or something? You know, if it's okay," he finished.

I muttered, "Yeah, I guess."

I continued to sit there while he fidgeted around, until,

obviously afraid of another invasion by my killer hippie mother, he said, "I guess we should get back."

As I slowly got to my feet and picked up my Walkman and book, he watched, waiting. It struck me that Gooseboy had very good manners, or at least a lot of courage, if he was waiting to walk me back to the gym and risk seeing my mother.

He held open the day-care door for me as I walked out into the hallway. Even with my massive headache, the squishiness was not gone. Together, but not talking, we made our way back to the gym. He wrote my phone number on his hand with a pen he produced from somewhere in his pants pocket. As I went to go inside, he held out his hand to shake mine. I fumbled my stuff into my other hand and shook.

The little bit of the auction I saw was interesting, even though my mind was on other things. Colin was the auctioneer, and he was really good. He would hold up a bag or a bowl of fish and people would bid on it. He tried to get the crowd to bid higher, the owner shouted out the merits of the particular fish, and the people laughed heartily and made a big show of enjoying themselves. Maybe they actually were. It's possible. I couldn't really tell.

MacGregor bid on a few things, and my mother tried to help him in between keeping her beady eye trained on me.

Mother, being Mother, didn't tell Geraldine and Pit about my little indiscretion. When we left the community center, I saw Gooseboy sitting under a tree in the picnic area next to the parking lot. He waved as I was getting in the car. I waved back. I then developed a bad case of goofy grin that I couldn't get rid of all the way home. It was very embarrassing.

Geraldine drove on the return trip, and for a hygiene-impaired person she actually didn't drive too badly.

I spent the time lost in *Dirty Dancing*–finale mode. Visions of our big number, Gooseboy in his boots, me in my stretch pants and headphones, wowing them senseless with our derring-do moves at the Alternative school dance flashed through my head. I could see my mother and father nodding approvingly, Death Lord breathing a big codependent caretaker sigh of relief, Aubrey falling in a heartbroken heap in some dismally lit corner, and Linda backing off in respect for Gooseboy's lack of grooming. It was a pretty good fantasy, and before I knew it, we were home.

I'm sure the fallout is coming. There is no way my mother will just let the little incident pass. Maybe if I tell her I've decided to become a sex educator, she'll attribute it all to some kind of work experience. I could say I want to be a sort of teenage Dr. Ruth, and the cloakroom thing was a kind of internship.

Later

Upon serious consideration, I have decided that this journal must be destroyed before I lose it or something. It would be just like me to forget it somewhere and make my

240

life even worse than it already is. Well, actually, my life isn't really that bad at the moment.

Gooseboy called this afternoon. He tried writing some poetry and showed it to his mother, who was encouraging but suggested that maybe that wasn't where his talents lie either. He asked if I thought he would be a good boyfriend. I asked him if he knew what a taxidermist was. I don't know. I think this relationship might be going somewhere. It turns out we are both interested in ranching. He has an aunt and uncle who live in the Kispiox Valley. He feels like he might be good at rounding up cattle and rodeos and stuff like that. So far they've only let him help with the haying, or at least they did until he was bitten by a field mouse hiding under one of the bales and had to be rushed to the nearest nurse's station for a rabies shot.

Maybe besides being a *Buffy*-watching, *Lord of the Rings*-reading cultural critic, I should make some future plans that will entail me getting my GED at age forty in the Kispiox, which is real ranch country. Perhaps I will be a cow milker for a living. Maybe we could live in the Kispiox and I could design gingham dresses and leather chaps—it would be a career choice that would make sense based on my career-testing diagnostic results.

I know I would want my profession to be separate from Gooseboy's ranching and rodeo pursuits. Particularly since, given his track record, his career might be quite short. I want to be an independent woman.

I wonder if he'll be threatened by the popularity and

success of my gingham dresses and chaps business? I wonder what exactly gingham dresses are? They sound like they would be popular with the Kispiox set. I wonder if there are enough people up there to set up my own sweatshop? I've discussed it with George, and she's willing to be a supervisor. We will need to get an employee somewhere. Maybe when Goose is on long-term disability from his rodeo riding, he could help. Us career girls have so many hard decisions to make. Bob is going to be so proud.